KILLING SIGNS

ERNEST MORRIS

GOOD 2 GO PUBLISHING

KILLING SIGNS
Written by Ernest Morris
Cover Design: Davida Baldwin – Odd Ball Designs
Typesetter: Mychea
ISBN: 9781947340428
Copyright © 2019 Good2Go Publishing
Published 2019 by Good2Go Publishing
7311 W. Glass Lane • Laveen, AZ 85339
www.good2gopublishing.com
https://twitter.com/good2gobooks
G2G@good2gopublishing.com
www.facebook.com/good2gopublishing
www.instagram.com/good2gopublishing

PROLOGUE

On this brisk February morning, the music rang loud throughout the night club as hundreds of partygoers danced to the sounds of Ella Mae. The music bounced off the walls and extended outside to the back alley, where Marcy was secretly celebrating her twenty-third birthday with Daryl in the front passenger seat of his Chevy Yukon. Unbeknownst to her, Daryl was a married man.

As he lifted up Marcy's black skirt and spread her legs to enter her, the passenger side window shattered across his back and into Marcy's face. The next swing from the crowbar knocked Daryl unconscious as it landed squarely on the left side of his temple.

"Please don't hurt me," Marcy screamed, coming down from the ecstasy high she was on.

Before she was able to scream again, she was also struck with the crowbar twice in the head. Their bodies were both gagged and duct-taped inside the

SUV. The attacker then jumped in the driver seat and drove off before anyone noticed what had transpired.

~ ~ ~

Early the next morning while traveling down interstate, heading to their early-morning church service out in Cleveland, Ohio, Raymond and Jeanine Kemp pulled off to the shoulder to see why the car was losing pressure in the front passenger-side tire.

"Be careful, Raymond," his wife stated, looking in the mirror.

Raymond exited the driver's side and walked around the back of the car, carefully watching for the oncoming traffic along the shoulder of the three-lane, rural, blacktop road. As he bent down to look at the tire, an eighteen-wheeler came whisking by, the force of the wind forcefully knocking him back and over the guardrail, into an embankment of gravel and bushes.

"Ouch!" he yelled.

He rolled about six to seven feet off the shoulder of the road, and on top of a woman's body. Raymond's eyes lit up at the gruesome sight before him. He immediately pushed himself up and raced back up the shoulder toward his car to call the police.

"What happened?" Jeanine asked, noticing the distressed look on his face.

"Oh God, darling, it's just awful," he said, dialing 911 on his cell phone.

Fifteen minutes after dispatch received the call, the interstate was full of Ohio state troopers and CSI investigators. Looking at the rigid state of the body and it's discoloration led them to believe that the woman had not been dead long. The lead trooper contacted Homicide and ordered his men to sweep the area in search of any evidence that may have been left behind. About twenty yards away from the first crime scene was another gruesome sight. A male's body lay dead, with his left arm decapitated. CSI took pictures of the surrounding area, and of the bodies. The female was wearing a red blazer, black skirt, white silk blouse, black mesh stockings, gold diamond studded earrings, gold heart necklace, and Apple watch. The male victim wore tan khakis, a black fitted shirt, black shoes, and a Rolex watch with diamonds inside.

Clutched tightly in the male's right hand was a section of a newspaper. It was the Aquarius horoscope. The passage said:

You've seen too much of life to have a strictly gloomy outlook. You know the shadow of darkness is there, and you're not afraid to peer into its dark eyes. Never let this darkness scare you . . .

Det. Lee was reading the piece of paper just as her partner and the medical examiner walked up from behind. The medical examiner told them as much as she knew, while they watched the bodies being loaded into the back of the van.

"I'll be able to tell you more once we get both bodies back to the morgue," the medical examiner said.

"No one is to speak to the press just yet. I want to be sure of the COD first."

ONE

It should have been invigorating, jogging at dawn, breathing the cool briny mist. But her morning run didn't work its usual magic. A hot shower didn't help clear her mind, nor did the cup of coffee she sat on her bed drinking, the smell of her lover still serenading her nostrils as she felt a tingling sensation between her legs. Her memories from last night were all so vivid, especially the way he gave her orgasm after orgasm.

Breathing in deeply, she closed her eyes to envision his face once again. Lying back on her bed, she caressed her breasts enough to make her nipples hard. Just thinking about his tongue caused her panties to become moist. She was about to slide a finger inside to release herself, when her cell phone rang.

"Damn, no time for fun. I'm late for work," she

mumbled to herself, answering the call as she rushed over to her closet.

By the time she arrived at her office building, she could see that everyone was busy running around with some kind of breaking news. One of her colleagues that was typing away on her computer signaled her over to where a conversation was being held.

"Sarah just posted a breaking news update online with what we know from the police and now the DA, which is little. A twenty-three-year-old female celebrating her birthday, and a male were found dead on the side of the road this morning. They won't say anything else about it until the press conference this afternoon." Marcus scribbled in black marker as quickly as he talked.

"Wow!"

"Sarah will be handling that. I think our editorial should focus on how the DA and police are being so damn tight-lipped. We've got a double homicide, and they want us to keep quiet. The DA only released a two-sentence statement to match the last two-sentence statement from police. I really think something more is going on and the public needs to know about it."

"Well, Sarah, you need to get a crew ready and get down to Central Detectives for the press conference. The rest of us will see what we can find out until then," Elaine stated as her cell phone vibrated.

Elaine walked away from the group looking down at her phone. She was hoping that her team would be able to get something out before the other news outlets could. She walked into her office and sat behind her desk. Her computer screen was showing a bunch of emails, coming from her informants. Her cell phone went off again just as she was about to read an article. A smile fluttered across her face.

"Hello!"

"Hey, sorry I had to rush off this morning. I'll make it up to you. Anyway, I have reservations at the Rock and Roll Hall of Fame tonight if you're free."

Elaine smiled, sitting back in her seat. Even if she wasn't free tonight, she would be now just to see the infamous Tony McAndrew again. He was the CEO of a startup company called BBB (Beauty Beyond Recognition). It was a magazine focusing on men and women that never get the recognition they deserve because of their weight and other misfortunes. They met at an exhibit she attended last months

"I'd like that."

"Good. How about I pick you up around seven?"

"I'll be ready."

"Okay, see you then. By the way, what are you wearing right now?"

"Well, I'm at work, so I guess clothes," she replied sarcastically. She could hear him chuckling on the other end. "I have on a skirt and blouse, why?"

"Are you wearing any panties underneath that skirt?"

"Yes I am, why?" she asked, shifting in her seat at the thought of the question. She could hear his breathing getting heavier through the phone, and that's when it hit her what he was doing. "Oh my, are you playing with yourself while you're talking to me?"

"Why don't you do the same. As a matter of fact, take off your panties right now and pull up your skirt. You're going to make yourself cum while I listen."

"What? Are you serious?" she replied, whispering like someone was in the room with her. "I'm at work right now. I can't do that. Somebody might walk in on me."

"That's the excitement of it. Knowing that at any

moment you could be caught. Now take them off and place the phone down there on speaker so I can hear the sound of your fingers going in and out."

"You are crazy, you know that? Hold on," she said. Elaine stood up, walked over to the door, and slightly cracked it. After seeing everyone doing their work, she closed the door back and locked it. She walked back over to her desk and removed her panties. "Hello! Now what do you want me to do?"

"I told you what I want you to do. Take off your panties," Tony replied.

"They're already off."

Elaine could feel her clitoris throbbing as she damn near came from the sound of his voice. She slowly followed his instructions, placing her legs spread eagle on top of her desk. With the speaker on, she placed a finger over her clit and begin moving it around in circular motions. Instantly her juices flowed down all over her hand. She stuck one, two, and then three fingers inside of her vagina, moving them in and out with precision.

Elaine got so into it, that she forgot she was in her office. She started moaning loudly as she sped up the pace. Not only was Tony enjoying the squishy sounds coming from the erotic session they were having, but also he was enjoying Elaine's panting and moaning. It didn't take long before someone was knocking on her door. She quickly took her legs off the desk and stood up, fixing her clothes.

"Just a second," she yelled out, seeing her panties lying on the desk. She snatched them up and stuck them inside her drawer. When she opened the door, Monica and Jeff were there. "What's up?"

"We thought something was wrong with you. We heard a loud noise," Jeff told her.

"Oh yeah, I hit my knee on the desk, but I'm okay. Thanks for checking on me."

"You sure?" Monica said, trying to peek in

Elaine's office.

"Yes, I'm sure, now let's get back to work."

Elaine closed the door and took a deep breath. She walked back over to her desk and picked her cell phone up off the chair. Tony had hung up but left a text message for her. When she opened the message, it was a picture of him naked and the words "See you tonight" in bold letters.

"Damn right you will." She smiled.

She needed to clear her mind so she could get back to the task at hand. Taking her panties out of the drawer, she used them to wipe herself and then tossed them into her purse.

~ ~ ~

Sarah and a bunch of other reporters waited in the crowded reception area at the Criminal Justice Center, better known as CJC, for the district attorney and chief of police to hold their news conference. They had switched the location due to scheduling conflicts. She hustled to get a seat in the first of three rows of chairs that were placed around the area. Her team of cameramen along with other crews were setting up their tripods in the back and strung them to eight microphones they attached on top of a wooden podium.

DA Cynthia Young walked in moments later, and stood behind the microphones. She was flanked by Chief Myers and men and women including department heads from Homicide and the Special Prosecution Unit that handled high-profile cases. The DA adjusted a few of the microphones, cleared her throat, and thanked everybody for coming. The roomful of reporters watched expectantly.

In a span of about five minutes, she recapped the brief statement her office and the Pennsylvania State Troopers had sent to the news crews earlier.

"The investigation is ongoing. Anyone with information should call 911, or our Crime Stoppers hotline immediately. We are looking into potential similarities in other cases as well. Now for a few questions."

"What have you uncovered about the murders?" a woman's voice rang out.

"We are following up on every possible lead in the case, and that's why we need help from all of you."

"What about the medical examiner's report?" another voice spoke up. "Are there any leads on the suspect, or a person of interest?"

The DA sighed, but answered, "Not yet. No witnesses that we know of. That's really all I can release at this time. We are trying not to say too much until we have enough information to speak on."

"Do you think that maybe this was a crime of passion?" Sarah asked. No answer. "Can you at least tell us how they were killed?"

"All we can say is that the two victims were

abducted from another area, to be determined, and dropped off on the side of the highway." That was the last thing the DA said before walking away with a few reporters trailing her to the door. They were being closed-mouth about the situation, but Sarah knew there was more to it than they were telling them.

Detectives Morris and Lee were shaking their heads, knowing that the higher-ups were keeping this tight-lipped because the girl's family was rich. The truth was, she should have never been in that area of the city last night. Sarah noticed the look on their faces and wondered what they knew. She approached them just as they were heading out.

"Detectives, this is nuts and you know it." Sarah cut right to the point. "Two people murdered in the middle of the night, and y'all are acting like you don't know what happened. What's really going on, and what aren't you saying?"

Det. Morris stayed composed, his strong jaw set, but his brown eyes smiled. He tilted his head to the side and looked over toward his partner before speaking.

"The girl's family is very wealthy, and due to their very generous donations, they are keeping everyone from talking." The whole time he spoke, he never took his eyes off Sarah. She noticed his look and started blushing.

"The families are difficult, I'm sure. And they have to be putting the pressure on to keep this quiet," Sarah answered quickly, feeling the butterflies form in her stomach. "Is that why the DA took over media relations from Mansfield PD?"

The only reply she got was a smile. Getting nowhere, Sarah switched the subject and asked the detective for an interview at a later time, not realizing that she just propositioned a date. He gladly obliged.

"Well I guess I've said too much already. I will

see you tonight at eight?" Sarah gave him a nod, agreeing and walked out of the courthouse.

~ ~ ~

The stocky man with the salt-and-pepper hair felt lightheaded as he crossed beneath the marble arch into the park. He had just left the bar from drinking after a hard day's work and needed to get home. He took off his circular glasses and blotted the sudden tears in his eyes with the sleeve of his suit jacket. He hadn't planned on breaking down, but the thought of seeing his wife sexing someone else still had him at a loss for words. Two years of marriage had suddenly been exonerated by a moment of weakness. Once he was finish sobbing, he crossed the street and decided to hand out more of his business cards before he hit his block. A few people were out enjoying the brisk weather.

"Hi there," he said, offering his business card to a young black woman pushing a toddler in a stroller.

He smiled at her, making eye contact. He had always been good with people, but not tonight.

"Leave me the hell alone with that nonsense," she said with surprising vehemence, almost smacking the card out of his hand.

He had to expect a little bit of resistance; after all, it was nine o'clock at night, and there were some creepy people lurking in the area. Unfazed by her reaction, he apologized and kept it moving down the street. The lady stared at him dumbfounded until he was out of sight.

Jeremy Duncan was a freelance photographer whose work was very well known on social media and other outlets. He had a reputation for taking exquisite photos and posting them online for all to see. For the right price, you could even hire him to spy on your spouse, and he would do it discretely.

As he walked past a driveway, he could see a figure lying on the ground squinting in pain. Without thinking twice, he rushed over to help them.

"Are you okay? Do you need an ambulance?"

He leaned over to see where the person was injured, and felt a sharp pain in his leg. Thirty seconds later his vision became blurry. The person he thought was injured suddenly stood up. Jeremy tried to move but couldn't feel his feet. Before he knew what happened, his vision turned from blurry, to darkness. His body was dragged into an awaiting car and taken away.

~ ~ ~

Bound in the dark, Jeremy thought about all the things he would give for a shower. Unidentified mud-like filth stuck to his T-shirt and boxers as he lay on the soiled concrete floor in a very tight space. An angry industrial hum raged in the vague distance. He was blindfolded, and his hands were cuffed to a pipe behind him. A gag around his mouth was knotted tight against the hollow indentation at the base of his skull.

The last thing he remembered was trying to help someone that looked like they were hurt and feeling a little sting in his leg. First he thought he had been bitten by something, but that was far from the truth. His memory seemed to stop at that point. How he got from there to here was still a mystery. For the millionth time, he tried to come up with a scenario in which everything turned out all right. He wondered where his clothes were and why was he half naked. He thought that maybe this was his wife's lover trying to get him out of the way so he could have her all to himself.

The scenarios in his head were too black to allow light to enter. He couldn't fool himself. He was in some deep shit right now. He banged his head on the pipe he was chained to as he heard a sound. It was the distant boom of a door. He felt his heart boom with it, in anticipation of what was to come. His breath didn't seem to know if it wanted to come in or go out.

He was pretty much convulsing when he made out a jangle interspersed with the steady approach of footsteps. He suddenly thought about the janitor in his building and thought he was about to be saved. It gave him hope.

"Hppp!" Jeremy screamed from behind the gag.

The footsteps stopped. A lock clicked open, and cool air passed over the skin of his face. The gag was pulled off.

"Thank you! Oh, thank you! I don't know what happened. I—"

Jeremy's breath blasted out of him as he was hit in the stomach with something tremendously hard. It was a steel-toed boot, and it seemed to knock his stomach clear through his spine. His head scraped the floor as he heaved in pain. At that moment, he knew this person wasn't here save him, but to harm him.

He had to think of something quick if he planned on getting out of there alive.

"Listen, I have money if you want it. Please, just let me go."

Jeremy panicked and twitched violently as the barrel of a stainless steel pistol softly caressed his right cheek. The pistol jabbed hard into his face, the hammer cocking with a sharp click. It was at that moment that he realized he wouldn't be walking away from this in one piece. He didn't even know who had kidnapped him.

"What do you want from me?" Jeremy yelled.

"Nothing you need to worry about," his captor replied before pulling the trigger. Jeremy's body went limp as his head dropped into his chest.

Blood began pouring out of the side of his head and onto the concrete. Not done yet, his captor did the unthinkable and severed his right arm.

TWO

"Yesss, right there. That feels so good. Don't stop!" Sarah moaned while Eric continued slurping away between her legs. Her eyes were closed and her hands caressed the back of his bald head. Eric ate her pussy like it was sirloin steak, not ignoring one spot.

Sarah had been with a few guys, but never had she experienced this kind of pleasure before. Especially from a black man. She had heard stories about how good they were in bed, but now to her satisfaction, she was getting a first-hand lesson. It was the best oral sex of her life. If his tongue could do this to her body, she couldn't wait to see what kind of performance his ten-inch penis would do.

"Oh my goodness, let me please you now," she blurted out, trying to push his head away from her vagina. He kept a firm grip on her legs so she couldn't escape.

"Tonight is all about taking care of you. I'll get

mine later."

A few hours ago, they had enjoyed each other's company by going out to dinner. Come to find out, they both had so much in common. Both were fans of the Cleveland Cavaliers and the Browns. They both had just gotten out of toxic relationships and weren't looking for anything long term yet. So after dinner they decided to let go and be free for the night. Eric invited Sarah back to his apartment for a nightcap, and she accepted, needing some affection.

"Stick it in please. I want to feel you inside of me," she moaned, spreading her legs as far as they would let her.

Eric couldn't believe how good her pinkness looked. It was glistening from both of their fluids. He pushed her legs behind her head and slowly entered her wet hole. He took his time because he knew she wasn't use to something so big. Sarah reached out grabbing his back and pulled him deeper inside to let him know she wasn't scared. In one swift motion, Eric flipped her over in the doggy-style position.

Eric plunged into her with such a force that Sarah had to gasp for air. After the initial thrust, she took it like a pro. Eric was amazed how wet she became from each stroke. When him and his wife were together, their sex life was never this good. He continued thrusting away until Sarah squirted all over his abdominal area and down his legs.

"I'm about to cum," he moaned, breathing heavily. Seconds later, he released his semen all over her back and buttocks.

"That was just what I needed, " Sarah panted, lying on her stomach for a minute to catch her breath. She turned over, staring into Eric's eyes as he leaned down and planted a gentle kiss on her lips. "I guess that means they'll be a round two?"

"I think I can accommodate that," Eric replied, kissing down her body until he reached her love tunnel.

He spread her lips apart and went back to work, trying to give her a record-breaking sixth orgasm. Just as he felt her body starting to tremble, his cell phone rang. Usually he would have let it go straight to voicemail, but it was the ringtone that made him stop. It was an all-broadcast call. The only time they got those calls was when a homicide was committed. He quickly answered the call. After a few yeses and head nods, Eric ended the call. Sarah had already gotten out of the bed and was getting dressed.

"No need to explain, work calls."

"How about we pick up where we left off after I'm done? That way I can make this brief distraction up to you without any more interruptions."

Before she could reply, he grabbed her ass, pulling her into his chest, and gave her a passionate kiss. Sarah could feel his nature rising all over again and pulled away.

"Sure! Now let's go before you start something you won't be able to finish."

"Be careful," Det. Morris told her.

Soon as she bent the corner, she pulled over to call her job, knowing that wherever he was going, a big story was sure to follow.

"Hey, I need a crew on standby. Something else just happened. Maybe it's another murder."

"Okay, where do you need them?"

"I'll text you when we get there," she replied as the detective drove past, sirens blazing. She ended the call and pulled off trying to keep up with him without being too conspicuous.

Ten minutes later, they arrived at an apartment complex near the Cleveland Museum of Art. There were officers all over the place, combing the area for evidence. Sarah watched from her car as the detective stepped out and was met by his partner.

"What happened?" Det. Morris asked, heading inside the building to see the body.

"We have a Caucasian male, believed to be in his late thirties. He was handcuffed to a pipe down here in the basement before being beaten and shot once in the head. They then tried to set him on fire, but not before cutting his right arm off," Det. Lee told him. "It was a good thing the smoke detector went off and the janitor was able to put the fire out before it destroyed all the evidence."

"Did anyone interview him yet?"

"I have a uniform taking his statement outside."

"Our last vic had a limb amputated, right?" Det. Lee nodded. "So someone is out here murdering people and removing body parts. What are they doing with them?"

"I don't know, but this is starting to have serial killer written all over it." They headed back outside so the CSI Unit could do their job. "How the hell did the press get here so fast?" Amanda asked when they stepped outside. Eric turned and looked in the direction she was pointing. He shook his head in frustration as Sarah and her news crew headed in their direction.

"I'll take care of this," he replied, walking away.

"What can you tell us about the murder, Detective?" Sarah wasted no time asking the first of many questions to come.

"What are you doing here?" He pulled her to the side so they could talk privately.

"Last I checked, I was doing my job," Sarah shot back. "And before you even begin with another accusation, no, I did not follow you. I received a call from my boss on my way home. If there's a problem, she's the one you should be talking to."

"Whoa, whoa, lil lady. Don't get so feisty. I was just asking a question. I thought you missed me already." He smirked. Sarah suddenly calmed down and gave him a smile of her own. He leaned in close to her ear. "Seeing you looking so beautiful makes me wanna rip those clothes off of you and take you right here and now."

"Down, tiger! Play your cards right and you'll get that chance later on."

"Well in that case, let's both get back to work before they start getting suspicious. We will be giving a brief news conference in a few minutes, but won't be answering any questions."

Sarah headed back over to her crew while Eric walked back to where his partner was standing. By this time, there were now multiple news crews on the scene, waiting on a story, and the mayor had just pulled up, which sparked a whisper on who the victim was. After giving the reporters an update on the homicide and being confronted by the mayor and their captain, Det. Lee and Det. Morris headed back to the station to put together a report, hoping to find a link between the two murders.

THREE

It was a close game as the two high schools competed for first place in their division. A deafening chaos of bouncing basketballs, screaming cheerleaders, and howling sugar-crazed kids rolled over the laminated hardwood floors. In addition to the noise, it was overly hot, dusty, and crowded, and Eric couldn't have been happier.

He found himself where he always did when chaos was present, smack dab in the middle of it. With a whistle around his neck, he was standing at center court, overseeing layup and passing drills as the two teams warmed up for the second half of the game. He found himself nodding in the affirmative when the principal asked him to officiate a couple of games this season. At first he'd been reluctant, but Felicia could smell a sucker like him from two miles away. It didn't help that they were high school sweethearts either.

The crowd had become so loud once the second

half started, that he didn't hear his phone ringing on his hip for the fifth time. Soon as they called a timeout, Eric checked and saw all the missed calls. He didn't recognize the number as work, but that didn't mean much.

"Detective Morris here," he screamed into the phone.

"Eric, it's Carol."

Carol was his new boss. Well, his boss's boss actually. Her name was chief Carol Jones. She was the commanding officer of the CPD's Special Investigative Division, which would have been a big deal even if she weren't the first woman to hold the job. Carol wasn't very popular around the department, because everyone knew she got the position from lying on her back with the big wigs.

"What's up, boss?"

"We have a possible kidnapping. You need to get back to the station and speak with a Mrs. Bennett. I know you're at the basketball game, but we just want to make sure it's not connected with our other cases."

"Who is this missing person?"

"Her name is Samantha. She just came back home from California seeing her father. She stopped at a gas station, and no one has seen or heard from her since," Carol stated before continuing, "I know what it sounds like, Eric, but I still need you to check it out. Get back to me as soon as you can."

Eric ended the call and waved over one of the referees. He walked over shaking his head, already knowing what he was going to say.

"Work calls, huh?"

"Yeah, I'm sorry, but y'all going to have to run a two-man show. I need to go check on something, hopefully very quickly. Can you handle it?"

"We got this. Go ahead and take care of your shit," his friend replied, blowing his whistle indicating the ball was back in play.

On his way back to the station, Eric decided to stop by Samantha's house. He parked around the corner from the Bennett's home. If in the unlikely case this was a kidnapping, it already could be under surveillance. He definitely did not want to advertise that the family had contacted the police. He passed through a wrought-iron gate and walked up the double-wide entryway. The heavy brass barred door opened as he reached the top. A poorly Asian doorman in a hunter-green suit stood at attention.

"I'm here to see Mrs. Bennett," Eric said, discreetly showing him his shield.

"It's Ms. Bennett. I've been divorced for quite some time now."

A stunning black-haired woman that looked no more than about thirty appeared behind the butler. Eric couldn't keep his eyes off of her petite frame. She was wearing a pair of black jogging pants that fit snugly against her curves, and a sports bra. Her hair was pulled back in a ponytail, and with no makeup on, she was drop-dead gorgeous. The agony on her lovely face was unmistakable though. Eric's annoyance at being called in dissipated as his heart went out to her. You could tell she was a concerned mom sick with worry.

"Thank you for coming Detective Morris, is it?"

"Yes, but you can call me Eric."

"And you can call me Veronica. Anyway, it's my daughter, Samantha. Something's happened to her."

"I'm here to help you find her, ma'am," he said as reassuringly as he could while taking out his notebook. "I just have to ask a few questions to get started. When was the last time you talked to your daughter?"

"I spoke with her last night when her plane arrived at the airport and after she picked up her car from the garage. She said she needed to stop at the gas station to pick up something. She never called or came home, and that's unlike her."

Maybe she met up with her boyfriend and stayed the night, he felt like saying to her.

"Not seeing someone for a few days might not

necessarily mean something's wrong, Ms. Bennett. Is there a specific reason why you think something's happened to her?"

"Her twenty-third birthday was yesterday, and we had planned on surprising her by taking her to her favorite restaurant. You don't understand how close we are. She would not have missed a chance of being smothered with gifts and being around her family and friends."

Eric was starting to understand her concern. What she was telling him did seem strange.

"Did she say anything to you when you last spoke to her? Anything odd? Someone new she might have met or maybe . . ."

That's when her phone sitting on the fireplace rang. Veronica stared in horror at the caller ID number and at the detective as it continued to ring.

"I don't know that number," she said, raw panic in her voice. "I don't know that number!"

"That's okay," Eric replied, trying to calm her

down. He scratched down the number and let his instincts kick in. "Listen, Veronica. Look at me. If it's someone involved with Samantha being gone, which I don't think it is, you need to ask them exactly what you need to do in order to get your daughter back, okay? And if you can, say that you want to speak to her."

Tears began to stream down her face as the phone rang again. She used a shaking fist to wipe them away before answering the call. Eric directed her to press record and put it on speaker so he could listen.

"Yes, this is Veronica." There was a moment of silence. "Who is this?"

"I have your daughter," a strangely serene voice said. You could tell that whoever called was using some type of voice-distorting device. "Listen!"

"Mom, please help me," a scared voice, immediately being recognized as Samantha's, yelled.

"You'll receive instructions in exactly three hours," the calm voice said. "Follow them to the letter or you'll never see your daughter alive again. No police. No FBI."

The connection was cut. Ms. Bennett kneeled down on the hardwood floor, sobbing inconsolably. Eric tried to pull her up, but she wouldn't move.

"It's Samantha," she moaned. "That bastard has my baby."

Eric helped her up onto one of the chairs and dialed his boss. Unbelievable. It really was a kidnapping he thought to himself. Her phone went straight to voicemail. He called again.

"C'mon," he said in frustration. "Pick up."

"We have to do something," Ms. Bennett said hysterically. She stood up and frantically walked toward the door, but Eric jumped in front of her. "Get out of my way. I have to find my baby."

"Trust me, ma'am, I'm going to do everything in my power to return your daughter home."

Veronica began sobbing and pounding on his chest. Eric held her tightly until her sobbing subsided. He looked into her eyes, wishing there was something he could do to ease her pain. They both began to feel the tension radiating off of their bodies, and Eric backed away not wanting to take advantage of her while she was in this state of mind. It was that moment that Veronica realized she needed a quick release. She reached out, grabbing for his belt buckle. He moved her hand away, backing up against the door.

"Detective, I know you're trying to help me, but right now I just need to feel you inside of me," she whispered into his ear as she moved in close once again.

In one swift motion, Veronica had his belt loosened and his khaki pants down to his ankles. She reached inside of his boxer briefs and removed his erection. Eric didn't know if he should accept the advance or run away. Once her lips covered his penis, all rationality went right out the door. She spit on the tip of his dick and ran her tongue up and down its length, letting her saliva cover his shaft entirely. When she took him into her mouth, it was warm and wet. Eric glanced down at her and was taken aback at how easily she deep throated him.

"We shouldn't be doing this. Oh my God," he moaned with his eyes shut. He leaned his head back against the door and grabbed her head, guiding it back and forth.

"Should we go up to my bedroom?" Veronica asked, releasing her grip on his manhood and standing up. He pulled up his pants, hesitating momentarily.

When Eric didn't answer, she took him by the hand and led him up the marble stairs, down the long hallway, and into the master bedroom. His eyes lit up at how huge the room was. Eric looked around at the different pictures that decorated the walls and didn't see any signs of her ex-husband. There were only pictures of her, her daughter, and another woman who he assumed was her sister. When he turned back around, Veronica was lying on the king-size bed buck naked with a smile on her face. She opened her legs just enough for Eric to get a perfect view of her pink pearl sticking out. She beckoned for him to come to her, patting the empty side of the bed.

"I'm so sorry, but I really think this would be very unprofessional for me, or should I say us, to do at a time like this. I need to get ready for when they call back," he said, leaving the room. Closing the door behind him, he leaned back on the wall and sighed.

FOUR

"I wanted you to see this before I removed it," the ME said to Det. Lee, pointing at something inside the victim's mouth.

Det. Lee walked over to the table where the body was, to get a look at what the medical examiner was talking about. Just like the other vic, this one had another horoscope message. The only difference was, instead of him having a piece of paper in his hand, it was written on his tongue. It was the Pisces sign with the quote: "Enjoy today, because tomorrow is never promised . . ."

"I've already sent pictures of it to your phone," the ME stated. "Does that mean anything to you?"

"I don't know yet. What I do know is, my boss is catching a lot of pressure from their boss, who is catching heat from the mayor. As you know, when shit hits the fan, everything rolls downhill."

"What ties does he have with the mayor?"

"Must be close because this case has taken

priority over all our other cases. Eric was supposed to meet me here but got stuck investigating a kidnapping that may be linked to these two also."

"What is going on in our city? Cleveland hasn't had this much drama since Lebron left the first time," the ME joked. "Soon people will be scared to come out of their homes."

"Girl, you ain't never lie. Don't worry, we will protect our city no matter what. If you'll excuse me for a moment while I update my boss on this new information."

The medical examiner went back to getting the corpse ready for transport to the funeral home. Det. Lee told her lieutenant about the message that was written on the dead man's tongue, and that she was going to follow up on a couple more leads before going home. As soon as she ended the call, Eric walked in holding a yellow envelope in the air.

"Guess what I have here?" he said smiling. "Too late, this here is a picture of our killer slash kidnapper."

"Wait, what are you talking about?" Det. Lee asked, snatching the photo out of his hand.

"Well after I left the Bennett's home, which, by the way, the lady is more worried about getting laid than finding her own daughter, I received a call from CSI. They found a print from a cup, about twenty yards from the first crime scene. Not the side of the road where the bodies were found, but the club they were at before being abducted. When we ran the prints through our database nothing came up, which meant they had no criminal history. So with the help of my federal buddy, we were able to run it through their federal database, and low and behold, we have a match."

"We need to get a bolo out on this person ASAP."

"Already done. I have the address right here." Det. Morris smiled, holding up a piece of paper.

"So what are we waiting for? Let's go grab this bastard before it's too late."

The two detectives rushed out of the coroner's office hoping to wrap this investigation up before dinner time. Det. Morris wanted to get back to the Samantha case. Somehow he believed that the two were connected, but something still wasn't adding up.

~ ~ ~

It was dark outside by time they arrived at the address Det. Morris had received. Along the way, he had called in for backup and SWAT. They had the house surrounded and were ready to move in by the time he and Det. Lee arrived.

"Let's get this son of a bitch," she stated, strapping on her Teflon vest and throwing on her windbreaker with the CPD logo on the back.

"Be careful and watch your back," Eric replied, pulling the assault rifle from the trunk of his vehicle.

Once everyone was in position, they stormed the home in search of their suspect. One man tried to reach for his weapon, but was immediately taken out. Officers cautiously approached the living room where Eliza was.

"Freeze, police!" the SWAT team commander

yelled out as his team infiltrated the room, guns aimed at the ready position just in case. "Keep your hands where I can see them."

By this time Det. Lee and Morris had also made their way into the room. Seeing that the threat had been contained, Eric walked up to Eliza and slapped the brass cuffs on.

"You have the right to remain silent," he began reading her rights. "Anything you say can and will be used against you in a court of law. You have the right to an attorney. If you cannot afford an attorney, one will be appointed to you by the court."

"I know my damn rights, you pigs."

"Where's the girl?" Eric replied.

"What girl? I don't know what the hell you're talking about."

"You think this is a fucking game, don't you? Maybe once we take you back to the precinct to meet your new roommates, you'll have a change of heart." Eric smirked.

"Fuck you," she replied, turning toward Eric and

spitting in his face.

"Get this piece of shit out of here now," Det. Lee said, passing her partner some tissue from her pocket to wipe his face. "Are you good?"

"Couldn't be better," he replied, giving her a high five.

"We got her. Now maybe the city can sleep a little better knowing that we got a killer off the street. We still need to find out why she did it, and where the girl is."

"We can do the interrogation together when we get back to the station, but for now, let's search every inch of this house." He turned to the other officers that were searching the immediate area. "I want this place turned upside down, and don't leave a stone uncovered. If she's here, we'll find her."

After doing a thorough search, they couldn't find any evidence of Samantha ever being there. However, they did find out the reason the man SWAT shot had tried to draw on them. There were bags and bags of ecstasy pills everywhere.

"Bag and tag every bag and send it back to the lab for processing," Det. Morris told a couple of uniforms.

"Shouldn't we call ATF or narcotics in?" a young rookie officer asked. "I mean, you guys are Homicide and this here is a drug case."

"Just do what you're told," Det. Lee snapped, leaving the officers there to collect the evidence.

~ ~ ~

"Two murders within a three-week span have the city of Cleveland in turmoil. Any other time, it would have been just another murder, but this was different. Somewhere out there is a psychopath, running around cutting off limbs of men and doing God only knows what with them. Authorities are no closer to a suspect than they were days ago. Anyone with information should contact CPD immediately. This is Warren Turner, reporting live from downtown Cleveland," the news reporter stated.

"This is getting out of control," Sarah said, lounging on the couch.

Eric walked in with two cups of coffee, handing her one before sitting next to her. They had been watching television, when Sarah decided to see what was on the local news. She loved seeing her competitors trying to break in a new story she had already released.

"Don't worry, we'll catch that son of a bitch," Eric replied, placing his cup on the coaster sitting on the coffee table. He placed Sarah's feet onto his lap and began massaging them.

"You sure know how to spoil a girl," she moaned, licking her lips.

"I can do more than that if you have time."

"I guess I will have to take a raincheck on that. I really need to get this story typed up for printing by morning."

Eric gave her one those seductive smiles and stood up in front of her. Already knowing what he was about to do, she shook her head mouthing the word no. He began unbuttoning his shirt, slowly pulling it off, giving her a striptease.

"Stop that!"

"What this?" Eric replied, unbuckling his belt.

He quickly slid out of his pants and briefs and stood there in nothing but a pair of socks. The sight of his naked masculine body had Sarah's panties moistening easily. He kneeled down in front of her, kissing her inner thighs through her pants, causing her to squirm just a bit. Suddenly the report she needed to do became an afterthought. She lifted his head and kissed him like a dog in heat. He pulled down her pants, along with her lace thong. The smell of her strawberry scent instantly made his stomach growl.

Eric flicked her clitoris with one finger while using his other hand to unsnap her bra, releasing her firm breasts from their captor. His tongue made its way from each nipple, down to her pussy. Sarah couldn't take it anymore, spreading her legs to give him all access to her sweetness. Eric slid her body halfway off the couch, lifting her buttocks in the air. The slurping and sucking sounds he was making sent her into an uncontrollable convulsion, followed by a humongous orgasm. Sarah didn't get a chance to catch her breath before he went right back to work. For the next few hours, they made love multiple times, exploring every part of each other's body. Eric did things to her that night that he hadn't done to any other woman, and she enjoyed every minute of it.

By the time Sarah woke up the next morning, she was exhausted. She heard Eric in the bathroom talking on the phone and walked over, putting her head against the door to listen. Hearing information about one of the cases she was working on, she took it upon herself to record the conversation. Soon as she heard him end the call, she rushed back over and got back in bed. Eric walked out dressed, ready to leave.

"I have to get to work. Something came up," he told her.

As soon as he was out the door, Sarah immediately got dressed and headed to the news station to share the information she recorded with her boss.

FIVE

S amantha Bennett was barefoot and wearing a blue-and-white Armani minidress when she was awoken by a thump against her hip, a bruising thump. She opened her eyes in the blackness as questions broke the surface of her mind.

"Where am I? What the hell is going on?" she thought to herself.

She wrestled with the blanket draped over her head, finally getting her face free and realizing a couple of new things. Her hands and feet were bound and she was in some kind of cramped compartment. Another thump jolted her, and she yelled this time.

"Hey!"

Her shout went unanswered, muffled by the confined space and the vibration of an engine. She realized she was inside the trunk of a car. It made no freaking sense to her! She tried telling herself to wake up from this dream she was having, but realization kicked in. She was awake, feeling the bumps for real, and so she fought, twisting her wrists against a knotted nylon rope that didn't give.

Samantha rolled onto her back, tucking her knees to her chest and, bam! She kicked up at the lid of the trunk, not budging it a fraction of an inch. She did it again, and again. The pain was shooting from her soles to her hips, but she was still locked up, and now she was hurting. Panic seized her and shook her hard. She was caught. Trapped. She didn't know how this happened or why, but she wasn't dead yet, or injured. Samantha vowed to do anything to keep it that way, and get away.

The last thing she remember before everything got fuzzy was getting off the plane, using the bathroom, and telling her mother she needed to make a stop before coming home. Wait, her mom must be worried sick, she thought. She needed to reach out to her somehow. Using her bound hands as a claw, Samantha reached around for a toolbox, a jack or crowbar, but she found nothing, and the air got thin as she panted in the dark.

Samantha tried to search again for her last memory, but her mind was sluggish, as if a blanket had been thrown over her brain too. She could only guess that she'd been drugged. Someone had slipped her a roofie, but who? When?

"Hellllpppp! Let me out!" she yelled, kicking out at the trunk lid once again and banging her head against a hard metal ridge.

Samantha's eyes were filling with tears and she was getting mad now on top of being scared out of her mind. Through her tears, she felt a five-inch-long bar just above her. It had to be the interior trunk release lever, and she whispered, "Thank you, God."

Her claw-hands trembled as she reached up, hooked her fingertips over the lever, and pulled down. The bar moved too easily and didn't pop the lid. She tried again, pulling repeatedly, frantically working against her certain knowledge that the release bar had been disabled. The cable had been cut. Samantha felt the car wheels leave the asphalt. The ride smoothed out, making her think the car might be rolling over sand. She wondered if the car was going into the ocean, and was she going to drown in the trunk?

She screamed again, a loud, wordless shriek of terror that turned into a gibbering prayer: "Dear God, let me out of this alive, and I promise you . . ." and when her scream ran out, she heard music coming from behind her head. It was a female vocalist, something popish, a song she didn't know. Who was driving the car? Who had done this to her? For what possible reason?

Now her mind was clearing, running back, flipping through the images of the past hours. Samantha was starting to remember. She had stopped at a bar to grab a drink and use the ladies room. She remembered seeing ten missed calls from her ex-boyfriend, but never answered. Was he behind this? Did he finally flip and pay someone to follow her and put something into her drink? Suddenly she was pissed.

"Jeremy? Jeremy?" she shouted out of frustration.

As though God himself had finally heard her calling, a cell phone rang inside the trunk. Samantha held her breath and listened momentarily. The phone was still ringing, but it wasn't her ringtone. It was a low-pitched burr, not Halsey's "Bad at Love." She needed to get to it before it stopped. Samantha fumbled with the blanket, ropes chafing her wrists. She reached down, pawed at the flooring, felt the lump under a flap of carpet near the edge, and bumped it farther away.

"Oh no," she mumbled.

The ringing started again, and her frenzy was sending her heart rate out of control when she grasped the phone. It was an old model. The one right before the flip phones were invented. Samantha clutched it with her shaking fingers, sweat slicking her wrist. She saw the illuminated caller ID number, but there was no name, and she didn't recognize the number. To her, it didn't matter who it was as long as they helped her.

Samantha pushed the Send button, pressed the phone to her ear, and called out hoarsely, "Hello? Hello? Who's there?"

Instead of an answer, she heard singing, this time Future's "Where Ya At" coming from the car stereo, only louder and more clearly. He was calling her from the front seat of the car.

Samantha shouted over the music, "Jeremy? Jeremy, what the hell? Answer me."

No answer, and Samantha was quaking in the cramped trunk, tied up like a chicken, sweating like a pig, with Future's voice seeming to taunt her. Suddenly the music volume went down, and the car stopped. She held her breath in the dark and listened over the pulse booming in her ears. This time, it was an unfamiliar voice that spoke out to her.

"Actually, Samantha, or should I call you Sam? It's kind of funny that you were so easy to catch. I thought it would be just a bit harder."

Samantha didn't recognize the voice. A new kind of fear swept through her like a cold fire, and she started to pass out, but got a grip on herself and stayed awake.

She tried replaying that voice in her head, hoping she would recognize it, but couldn't. Everything she'd envisioned she would say to Jeremy if it was him, was now all gone. The truth was, a stranger had abducted her, tied her up, and thrown her into the trunk of his car. She'd been kidnapped, but why? Her mother was probably sick with worry right now. Samantha listened in silence before asking a question.

"Who is this?"

No one answered. The line disconnected. Then the thoughts tumbled in her mind. She realized she was still gripping the phone. She held the keypad to her face, barely able to read the numbers by the pale light of the faceplate. She managed to dial 911. She listened to the three rings and four, and then the operators voice.

"Nine-one-one. What's your emergency?"

"My name is Samantha Bennett. I've been—"

"I didn't get that. Please spell your name."

As soon as Samantha tried to speak again, the

phone went black. The battery had died on her, sending all hope of being rescued out the door.

"No," she yelled out, pressing the power button to no avail.

Suddenly the car came to an abrupt stop. She could hear keys being fumbled around and one being inserted into the trunk's lock. The trunk lid lifted, and sunlight spilled over her face. Samantha hauled back her knees and kicked hard at the man's thighs. He jumped back, avoiding her feet, and before she could see his face, a blanket was thrown over her head. She never even had the chance to scream, as the prick of a needle pinched her in the thigh. She heard the voice as her head rolled back and the light faded.

"You shouldn't have done that."

As he was about to remove the body, someone approached him from behind. He turned around just in time to see who it was.

"I was just about to call you. I did everything you asked me."

Before he could finish his statement, two bullets entered his heart, killing him instantly.

SIX

R ing, ring! Ring, ring!

"Hello," Eric answered in a groggy voice.

"Wake up, partner, our killer has struck again. Meet me under the Fulton Bridge."

Eric ended the call and checked the time. It was only two in the morning. Last thing he remembered before dosing off to sleep was talking to Veronica Bennett and watching the highlights of Philadelphia Eagles losing to the New Orleans Saints. He quickly hopped out of bed and got dressed. After brushing his teeth and washing his face, Eric headed over to the crime scene to see who their latest victim was.

"I thought you might need this," Det. Lee said, passing him a hot cup of coffee when he stepped out of his vehicle.

"Thanks! What do we have?" he replied, taking a sip.

There were crime scene investigators everywhere collecting evidence. Eric followed her over to where the body was covered with a sheet. There was a trail of blood, which told him that the body had been moved from its original spot, but it wasn't moved far. There were also two sets of tire tracks, letting him know that two vehicles were there.

"Who found the body?" Eric asked, lifting up the sheet to see the man's face. He had been shot twice in the chest and left to die under a bridge.

"Some homeless man was looking for a spot to sleep for the night when he stumbled across him. He called 911 after searching his pockets for money." Det. Lee smiled. "He's over there giving a statement to the officers."

"What does this have to do with our case? Why not give it to someone else?" he asked, looking over to his partner, who scooted down beside him.

She pulled the sheet down some more, and that's when he saw it: on the man's stomach was another quote from a horoscope. This time it was a quote from the Aries sign. Det. Morris pulled out his cell phone to snap a few pictures of the message:

One-on-one relating suits you perfectly. You

might not get the results you desire, but you will come to terms with a difficult situation. Keep searching and you will find the answer you're seeking.

"I wonder why he's writing quotes from horoscopes."

"Maybe he wants us to solve the riddle," Det. Lee joked.

"Well let's help accommodate his wishes. It's time to put this asshole behind bars with the rest of the lowlifes," Eric told his partner as they headed back to their vehicles.

~ ~ ~

Elaine walked out of the bathroom buck naked, and wet from the shower she just took. Her body glistened from the morning sunshine that lit up the room through the open curtain. Tony was lying in the bed in a deep sleep, still trying to recover from last night's festivities. Instead of him working her out, it was the other way around this time.

They had planned to meet up last night, but

Elaine was running late because of some unexpected business she needed to tend to. When she had arrived at his home, Tony was a bit displeased by her tardiness, but that displeasure soon turned into lust. She wore a long coat with nothing on under it.

"Are you awake?" she whispered in his ear.

Tony yawned and looked up at how beautiful she was. In his mind, she would be the perfect soulmate if he wanted to get married and settle down. Everything about her said wifey material, but he wasn't ready for that kind of commitment yet.

"Yeah, I'm up! I need to take a quick shower. Would you like to join me again?" he asked with a smirk on his face.

"No, you go right ahead. I have to get ready for work."

"Suit yourself," he said, heading into the bathroom.

Soon as the door closed, his phone vibrated. Elaine looked down on the nightstand, noticing that he had a photo text. Curiosity got the best of her. She picked up the phone and opened the message.

"I know this motherfucker ain't fooling around on me. I'm tired of men lying and cheating like we're pawns in their little game," she snapped. There were four photos of a beautiful female lying in bed. Some were nude and some were in lingerie. "You're just like all the others."

Elaine looked at the nude pictures that were sent to his iPhone once again and placed the phone back on the table. She was dressed and ready to leave by the time Tony finished in the bathroom. The look on her face puzzled him.

"What's wrong?" he asked, confused.

"Nothing, I have to go. You should turn your phone off when you have company, or at least put a password on it," she said, walking out the door.

"Wait—"

Tony couldn't get his words out fast enough before the door shut in his face. He was about to chase after her and ask what the sudden change in her attitude was, but his phone buzzed again. He picked it up thinking that it was Elaine. Seeing all the photos that were sent to him by one of his many females told him everything he needed to know. He knew he fucked up by leaving his phone in the room. Any woman that hears her so-called boyfriend's phone ringing is going to get curious and check it. That was stupidity on his part.

"Fuck!"

SEVEN

"I need you to tell me right now what kind of progress you're making on this case. I have given you ample time to get me results, and I demand some answers," district attorney Cynthia Young snapped. Chief Myers and his two lead detectives had been summoned to her office earlier that morning, but he was just now arriving. She didn't look too happy about the situation either. He really didn't care anyway. The only reason he was there in the first place was because of his boss, the mayor. He had contacted them and told him to meet him at the DA's office ASAP. Now that he stood in front of them both, he felt like he was the one being interrogated. With a calm voice, he gave them a brief rundown of where they were in the case.

"I understand your concern in this matter, but I assure you that my two detectives are treating this case just like all the other cases that come across their desk."

"Stop right there," the mayor interrupted. "That's exactly what I don't want you or your detectives doing. I want y'all to treat this as an extra-sensitive high-profile case. We have a missing woman out there somewhere, and a pleading mother sitting at home worried sick to her stomach about her whereabouts."

"I don't think she's that worried," Eric mumbled, thinking about what almost happened.

"What was that, officer?"

"Nothing!"

"I thought so. Now, where are we with the evidence? Can I go to a judge right now to begin an indictment?" the DA asked.

"We're trying to connect the dots on a couple of homicides that we believe are tied to this abduction," the chief began. "The three victims are in some way—"

"So what can you two tell me about this?" the mayor cut in, interrupting the chief. He was staring at the two detectives, more so at Eric, who looked bored or like he had more important stuff to do instead of being there.

"Like the chief was saying, we have leads to follow, but we can't do our jobs if you keep calling us here for updates," Eric fired back, not caring that he was talking to people that could have him walking the beat somewhere. "I'm sorry if my words came off a bit harsh, but that girl is out there, and every second we are wasting trying to explain our actions is another second on her life."

"What my partner is trying to say is," Det. Lee cut in, "that we are using all of our resources to bring her home safely. Whoever has her hasn't called for a ransom or anything as of yet, but we're still being optimistic that they will."

Seeing that he was wrong for holding the detectives back from finding the girl, the mayor excused everyone except Eric. Once they were out of the room, the mayor looked at the detective like he wanted to kill him.

"If you ever speak like that to one of your

superiors again, you will be writing tickets or worse—" he stated, not having to finish his statement because Eric immediately got the message.

Once he left the DA's office, he headed back over to the Bennett residence. The FBI had set up surveillance equipment and tapped her home and cell phones. Now they were just waiting for a call from Samantha or her captor. Despite the home being filled with law enforcement, Veronica still gave him lustful stares and paraded around the house in tight-fitting clothing. Eric tried to keep his composure, but it was getting difficult by the minute. He wanted her probably more than she wanted him. When he went to use the bathroom, she was getting something out of the closet. She felt him staring at her, so she bent over like she was picking up something, giving him a full view of her ass. He saw her pussy lips poking through the tights, indicating that she wasn't wearing any panties. The bulge in his khakis told her she was getting to him.

"Don't worry, I don't bite, unless you want me

to," she whispered.

Shaking his head, Eric walked into the bathroom, closing the door behind him. Just as he finished and was washing his hands, Veronica stepped in and locked the door. Eric was shocked by how fast she had dropped to her knees, unzipped his pants, and had her lips wrapped around his penis.

"We can't do this," he said, leaning back on the sink.

The sensation of her tongue had his knees buckling within minutes. He tried to pull out when he felt himself about to cum, but she held on to his waist. Seconds later he shot his load into her mouth. Veronica swallowed every drop of his semen. This time, instead of pulling away, he stood her up and bent her over the sink and pulled down her tights. He had to have her. Her pussy looked so good from the back that he felt himself about to cum again just from the sight of it. He entered her warm hole, slowly stroking it to find his rhythm.

"Oh my God, that feels so good. Go faster, baby.

I want to cum before someone catches us," she moaned, feeling her orgasm coming. "Harder, faster, yes, like that. I'm cuummmming."

Eric pumped away, giving her what they both wanted. She gripped the edge of the sink, and pushed back as the explosion took its natural course. Eric felt his own orgasm coming again and held onto her waist tightly, shooting his load inside of her. When he finally pulled out, his semen spilled out down her legs. She stood up and turned around. Looking Eric in the eyes, Veronica leaned in, kissing him softly on the lips.

"That's what I needed all this time. Now can we please focus on getting my daughter back?"

Eric couldn't respond to the sudden change in her demeanor. They both wiped off using washcloths on the rack and fixed their clothes before stepping out of the bathroom, one at a time. None of the agents even realized they had been missing. Veronica brought them something to drink just as a live video popped up on the computer screen the Feds were monitoring.

When everyone looked at the screen, Samantha was lying on her stomach. She was perfectly hogtied, her hands behind her back and tethered to her legs, which were bent up at the knees. Veronica was terrified at the state her only child was in.

"Samantha," she screamed out. Eric held her back as she tried to reach out to the screen. "Let me go!"

"Let us handle this, Mrs. Bennett. We need to find out what they want," one of the agents replied.

"No, I want him to handle it. I only trust him," she demanded, pointing to Eric.

He released his hold on her and gave the FBI agent a nod. Usually they wouldn't let non-federal officials take charge of their case, but due to the circumstances, they had no choice but to comply. Samantha could be seen pleading with her abductor. She was sobbing softly. Even though she couldn't see her mother, she knew she was watching.

"Please, please untie me. I just want to go home."

Her captor's face was transformed by the plastic mask and digitally altered voice. Both Det. Morris and the Feds were trying to figure out who was behind this kidnapping, and what their end game was. And then, just as they thought nothing else would happen, the masked assailant straddled her body, wrapping his hand in the young woman's long hair. He lifted her head from the flat of the bed, pulling hard enough that her back arched, and the force of the pull made her cry out in pain.

"I want $300,000 placed in the trashcan outside of the pizza store on Market Street. If you bring any cops, she dies." He released his grip and stood up. "Be there, alone at four o'clock sharp. Remember, no cops." The video ended, leaving them in a trance.

"Okay, I need you to go sign out the $300k from the 1505 funds, and tell them we just need it for flash," the lead agent told a fellow agent.

"There's no time for that," Veronica replied. "I'll get the money myself. Besides, I have to take it or he'll kill her."

"It's too risky," Agent Pride told her. "I can't have a civilian in the line of fire like that. We'll send one of our agents to the rendezvous spot dressed like you."

"He knows who she is, Jack. Her daughter's life is at stake here. He will smell a Fed from a mile away. We can't risk that."

"So what do you suppose we do, Eric?"

"Let her go, and I'll be right there with her. They'll never see me. We can put a tracker inside the bag and follow him back to wherever he is keeping Samantha. You can have some agents around the perimeter, but don't let them be seen."

"Okay, we'll try it your way, but if anything goes wrong, do not hesitate to get her out of there ASAP. Are we clear on this?" Agent Pride said, looking around the room at all of the other agents, especially Det. Morris.

Everyone nodded their heads in agreement and started getting ready. Eric pulled Veronica to the side so they could talk. When they were out of sight of the other officers, Veronica hugged him tightly as the tears flowed freely down her face.

"Are you sure you're up for this?" he asked with compassion.

"I think so, as long as you're there with me."

"I'll be right there. Now let's go get the money ready."

~ ~ ~

There were agents waiting everywhere for the drop to take place. Det. Lee and Morris sat inside the restaurant watching Veronica, who had just pulled up. When she stepped out of the car, she was wearing a pair of jeans that showed her every curve, knee-high boots, a light jacket, and a beanie hat. As she walked into the restaurant, all eyes were on her. Even Det. Lee had to admit how beautiful she was.

"You were right, it would have been hard to find someone to impersonate her in that little bit of time. She walked in this place, demanding attention."

"Yeah, let's just hope that attention doesn't get her killed," Eric replied.

"Look," Det. Lee said, pointing to the figure that just walked into the store. Whoever it was wore a hoodie and glasses so they wouldn't be recognized.

They walked straight back to the bathroom where the money was supposed to be. Two agents stood right outside the door waiting for the person to come out with the bag. There were also agents outside, watching the back exit just in case they snuck out that way. Five minutes went by and no one came out.

"Does anyone have eyes on the suspect?" Det. Morris spoke through the earpiece.

"Not yet."

"We're all clear out here," the agents watching the back replied.

"I'm going to go check the bathroom," Det. Morris said, getting up from his seat.

"No, just hold off for a second. We don't know if that was even the person we're looking for. Look, the bag hasn't moved yet," replied Det. Lee.

Eric looked over at the monitor she was holding in her hand, and just like she said, the bag was still there. Even though he saw it with his own eyes, something wasn't sitting right with him. He jumped up to head toward the bathroom, when the person wearing the hoodie walked out. Eric stopped in his tracks and acted like he was about to order something else from the counter.

"Do you want us to take him when he comes out?" the agent radioed to Eric.

"No, that's not who we're looking for. Let 'em go."

A few seconds later, Veronica's cell phone rang. She looked at the caller ID and answered.

"Hello!"

"Put the plainclothes officer that keeps staring at you on the phone." Veronica looked at Eric and held the phone out to him. Knowing they had been made, he walked over and took the phone out of her hand. "You officers must really underestimate me. Too bad the joke's on you."

The line went dead before he could respond to the caller. Remembering what the caller just said caused

Eric to sprint toward the bathroom. He grabbed and opened the bag of money.

"It's gone," he yelled, running out of the restaurant. "Does anyone have eyes on that person that left wearing the hoodie? They have the money. I repeat, they have the money."

Everyone gave negative responses as Det. Lee came running out behind him. Whoever that person was, was nowhere in sight. Eric and Sonya started walking back toward his vehicle, when it suddenly went up in flames. The explosion knocked him off his feet and into a parked car. Agents were scattering all over the place in search of the missing money and the person who took Samantha, while the rest attended to Eric, who was trying to get up off the ground.

"Relax, an ambulance is on its way," his partner said, scooting down next to him.

"This is all my fault. I never should have let that prick get away."

"It's not your fault, partner. If anyone is to blame,

it's that prick that got away," she told him, hoping the ambulance would hurry up and get there.

Even though he was right about it being his fault, Sonya would never say that to her partner. The guilt alone was eating at him right now. Samantha's abductor now had her and the money. There was no telling what he would do to her.

EIGHT

Elaine felt weightless in Tony's arms, like an angel. Her long legs locked around his waist, and all he had to do was raise his knees and she would be sitting on his lap. He did just that as they bobbed in the pool. She lifted her face to him.

"Tony, this has been the best."

"It gets better from here," he said.

She grinned at him and kissed him softly and deeply, a long, salty kiss followed by another, electricity arcing like heat lightning around them. He undid the string tie at her neck, jerking loose the tie behind her back. The bikini top easily slid from around her firm breasts. Elaine was too busy licking his ear to notice how hard her nipples were against his chest. She groaned as he shifted so she was pressed even tighter to him, rubbing like an eager beaver against his dick.

He reached around and ran his fingers under the elastic of her bikini bottoms, touching the tender places, making her squeal and squirm like a kid. She pushed down at the waistband of his swim shorts with the backs of her feet.

"Wait," he said. "Be good."

"I plan to be great," she sighed breathily, kissing him, pulling at his shorts again. "I'm dying for you."

Tony unhooked her legs and pulled off the bottom half of her swimsuit. Carrying the naked girl in his arms, he walked over to the shallow part of the pool and stepped out as water streamed off their bodies. She hung onto his neck as he took her over to where he had left his duffle bag. He stopped and unzipped the bag, and pulled out two enormous beach towels. Still balancing the girl in his arms, he spread out one towel and lay Elaine softly down, covering her with the second towel. She smiled as she watched him remove his shorts.

"Oh my God, oh my God, Tony, not right here."

"Why are you talking? Just lie back and let me drive this bus," he replied, giving her a smile of his own.

He knelt between her legs, tonguing her sweet spot until she cried out, "Please, I can't stand it, Tony. I'm begging you, please." Then he entered her.

Elaine's screams were washed away by her moaning and groaning, just as he knew they would be each time he filled her up with all ten inches. Each stroke was slow and sensual. It didn't take either one of them long to reach the climax they had been anticipating. He raked the back of her hair, kissed her closed eyes, put his arms around her naked frame, and warmed her up with his skin. Elaine laughed, snuggling up against his chest. It was the first time in a long time she had felt so comfortable around a man.

Elaine's magnet for men had led her to some disappointing relationships. They would either cheat on her, or simply have no expectations in life. When she met Tony, it only was supposed to be about sex, but as time went on, it progressed into something more. She was beginning to fall head over heels for him, and she thought the feeling was mutual. Whenever they couldn't see each other, they would

Facetime and have video sex. He helped her bring out her freakiest inhibitions.

"That was awesome," Elaine whispered with her eyes still closed. "I was just thinking, we've been seeing each other for a while now. I think you should have something."

She reached over, grabbing her purse. Tony sat up to see what she was doing. She pulled out a set of keys and passed them to him.

"I can't take these," he replied, passing them back to her. "What we have is strictly fun. We can't get caught up with feelings. It will only complicate things."

Hearing him say that made her want to run away and cry, but she held her composure. It was at that point that she realized the mistake she had made. She stood up and began putting her clothes back on.

"Come on, Elaine, where are you going?" She didn't respond. He stood up and grabbed her hand. "Stay for another round before you leave."

"No, sorry, but I have to go," she told him,

rushing out of the pool area.

"Elaine," he called out to her. "Elaine."

~ ~ ~

Veronica Bennett sat in a chair by the window in an emotional state of mind. Ever since the failed attempt to get her daughter back, she had not wanted to talk with anyone. Just as expected, Det. Eric Morris took the heat for the whole fuck-up. They found C4 underneath the police vehicle that exploded. They all wondered how the perp miraculously snuck out of the restaurant, planted a bomb, and snuck back in without anyone seeing him. This was a mystery to everyone, including Eric.

The FBI wanted him suspended for his mishap, but the higher-ups felt like that would be letting him off the hook too easy. Instead, they made him their personal errand boy. The kidnapper hadn't contacted them since taking the money, which most likely meant he was going to kill Samantha. As they were beginning to talk about their next plan of action, another live feed popped up on the computer screen, confirming their suspicions.

Everyone in the room was surprisingly quiet as the captor walked over to Samantha, straddled her body from the back, and pulled back her head using her hair for leverage. He picked up a serrated knife from beside him and made a deep cut across the back of her neck. The pain immediately caught up to her as a curdled scream erupted from her painted mouth. Samantha wrenched her body as her abductor sawed and cross-sawed through her muscles, and then the scream cut out, leaving an echo as her head was severed from her body in three long strokes.

"Get her out of here right now," Eric yelled, still watching the horrific sight. "She doesn't need to see this."

An agent quickly pulled Veronica out of the room as she kicked and screamed. The other agents continued watching the screen, some of their eyes tearing up.

Arterial blood spurted out against the white walls, emptied onto the satin bedsheets, ran down the arm and loins of the abductor kneeling over the dead girl. His smile was quite visible through the plastic mask as he held up Samantha's head by her hair so that it swung gently as it faced the camera. A look of pure despair was still fixed on her beautiful face. The killer's digitized voice was eerie and mechanical as he calmly spoke to the officers.

"I hope everybody's happy," he said. "You did this to her."

The camera held on Samantha's face for another long moment, and then the screen went black.

NINE

Jered headed to McDonald's to pick up some breakfast before heading to work. This was his normal routine every morning. After grabbing his food, he decided to take the long way to work to prepare himself for the hailstorm he would be walking into. As he was hitting the expressway, he never realized that he was being followed. The motorcycle kept it's distance, maintaining full visual on its target. Once they passed the next to last exit, the biker made its move.

Eighty miles per hour, ninety. The rider drifted right in behind the sports car, let go of the left handlebar, and grabbed the TEC-9 with the extended clip, Velcroed to the gas tank. The expressway was coming to an end, so the car would have to brake. The motorcyclist decelerated, dropped back, and waited for it. When Jered's brake lights came on, the motorcyclist hit the gas and made a lightning-quick jagging move that brought him right up next to the passenger-side window. Through the tint, only a silhouette of the driver could be seen. The shooter fired twice at Jered. The window shattered. The bullets hit hard.

Jered swerved left, smacked the guardrail, and spun back toward the inside lane just as the biker shot ahead and out of harm's way. He tried reaching for his gun, but couldn't control his vehicle. It smacked head-on, into a tree. He climbed out the window and fell to the ground. He could hear the roar of the motorcycle getting closer. This time, able to reach for his weapon, he fired three shots in the direction of the motorcycle, missing his intended target as it sped up. Jered went to reached for his phone, when a sharp pain infiltrated his side. His whole body went numb. A moment later, Jered caught red fire flashing in his peripheral vision, heard the whispering sounds of rapid pistol fire, and felt bullets hit him, one of them in his chest. It drove him back against his vehicle.

A passing pedestrian screamed but caught the next two bullets, falling to the asphalt. Blood was gushing out on the sidewalk everywhere. For Jered, everything became far away and slow motion. He fought for breath. It felt like he'd been bashed in the ribs with a sledgehammer. He could see other people running into buildings hysterically screaming. He went on autopilot when the motorcyclist got off the bike, and pretended he was dead. He could feel something being written on his forehead.

"Hey, get away from him. The cops are on their way," a man yelled from his car.

The shooter aimed the pistol in the direction of the driver, and he accelerated his vehicle trying to get out of the line of fire. Unexpectedly, the threat worked, causing the killer to hop back on the bike and flee the scene before they arrived. Jered managed to dial 911 from his phone.

"Nine-one-one, what is your emergency?" the female dispatcher asked.

"Officer down," Jered croaked. "Need backup at the warehouse district. I repeat, officer . . ."

He felt himself swoon and start to fade. He let go

of the phone and struggled to breathe. He could see that the other victim wasn't moving and his face looked blank and empty. Jered whispered to him before dying, "Sorry, sir," he said. "I'm so sorry."

~ ~ ~

Sarah sat at her news desk waiting to go live on air. She hadn't seen Eric since recording his conversation, and was really missing him. He wouldn't answer any of her calls.

"You're on in three, two, one," the camera guy said, counting with his fingers.

On cue, she began reporting the latest news, smiling, trying to hold back what she was feeling. Once off the air, she decided to pay him a visit. If their relationship was over, she needed to hear it straight from the horse's mouth so she could try to move on. She pulled up and parked outside of the police station.

Just as she was about to step out of her vehicle, Eric and another woman came strutting out. Sarah stepped out, slamming the door like a woman on a mission. A mission to murder.

"Eric, can I speak with you for a moment?" As she got closer, her mind eased up a bit. The woman that was walking with him was his partner. "Hello, Det. Lee!"

"You're that news reporter that miraculously arrived at our crime scene, right?" she asked Sarah, the whole time staring at her partner.

"Yes, that's me. It will only take a second, I promise."

"I'll meet you at the car," he told Sonya, walking to the side with Sarah. "What's up? I'm really busy with this kidnapping case, and, no, I can't discuss it right now. You will have to wait like the rest of the reporters."

"I didn't come here to talk about no case; I was just wondering why you haven't been answering any of my calls," she replied in a frustrated tone.

Eric knew why he hadn't called her back, but didn't know how to just come right out and say it. His problem was, he wasn't looking for anything exclusive right now. Sarah, on the other hand, wanted more than he was willing to offer. He loved the way his life was going, and relationships would only complicate things.

"It's kind of hard to explain right now, but maybe we could discuss it over dinner tonight? How about I pick you up around seven, and we can eat and talk?"

The thought of getting another chance to be with him gave her a reassuring feeling that there was still hope they would be together. Sarah didn't need to answer because her smile said it all. Suddenly, officers came running out of the station. It seemed like all hell had broken loose.

"Eric, we have to go now," Sonya yelled out the driver-side window. "We have an officer down!"

"I have to go."

Eric rushed around to the passenger side of the car. Whenever a fellow officer is in trouble, everyone in the immediate area responds.

Sonya hit the sirens, and they sped toward the warehouse district. They arrived at the scene within twelve minutes. Light rain had started to fall when Eric and Sonya climbed out of their unmarked car. It was only two thirty in the afternoon, and the humidity was already subsiding. The left side of the road was closed off for a medical examiner's van and two Cleveland State patrol cars and troopers. Afternoon traffic was going to be horrendous. The younger of the two officers nodded his head and pointed over to where two detectives were standing, talking.

"Thanks," Det. Lee said.

"We were just leaving the station when we heard the call. What do we have here?" Det. Morris stated as they walked up to where the bloody corpse was lying.

"Homicide. He was alive before he hit the tree. Must have climbed out in an attempt to get them before they got to him. Got a couple of rounds off before he died," one of the detectives replied.

"Reports of gunfire before the crash?"

"None that we know of," the other detective

chimed in.

When Eric knelt down and pulled back the sheet, his heart almost dropped to his feet. Eric had been on the force for ten years and seen hundreds of murder scenes. He usually got to work inside a suit of psychological armor that kept him at an emotional distance from all victims, but this time would be different. It was his longtime friend. He had trained him when he was a rookie in Philadelphia. After a year on the job, they both had transferred to Cleveland, Ohio, and gone their separate ways. This case had just become personal to him, and when dealing with murder, he didn't like it to be personal. Rational, observant, and analytical, that was his style, among other things.

"Is that Captain Ingram?" Det. Lee asked, standing over her partner. He nodded his head. "What the hell happened?"

"I guess our serial killer has struck once again. Look," he said pointing to the words written on the corpse's forehead.

The killer had started writing another horoscope quote, but didn't get the chance to finish. There was also a gash around Captain Ingram's torso area. Det. Lee knelt down to get a better look at it, while Det. Morris took pictures of it using his iPhone.

"You two were really close?"

"Yeah, if it wasn't for him, I wouldn't be the cop I am today. He taught me everything I know. When we came out here, we were supposed to work in the same precinct, but they promoted him to lieutenant," he said, staring at his mentor. "He told me that I would have to make my own way up the ranks without him being there in the physical. I used to go to his home for dinner with his wife and kids every Sunday, until he was promoted again, up to captain. Speaking of his wife and kids, I'll have to be the one to tell them."

"I can go with you if you want?"

A patrolman approached and laid out what seemed to have happened based on the initial statements he'd taken from witnesses. They said a motorcycle came alongside the car and opened fire. The car then crashed into a tree, and Captain Ingram crawled out firing at the cyclist. Chaos ensued, and a bystander was hit and another got away after yelling that he called the police. On that, all the witnesses agreed.

When there's gunfire involved, witnesses dive out of the way, trying to find cover or safety, which is entirely understandable. Folks have the right to survive, but fear and panic makes the detectives' job harder, because they have to be sure those emotions don't cloud their judgments or taint their memories.

Sonya and a couple of troopers continued to interview the witnesses, while Eric walked the perimeter of the crime scene looking for clues. Lying in the gutter about ten feet from the corpse was a military-issued rigid knife. Eric took some pictures of it before picking it up. Remembering the cut on the captain's torso, he knew this was his serial killer. This might be the biggest lead yet.

"What are you thinking, Eric?" Sonya asked.

"It's kind of strange. The officers said they asked witnesses if they heard gunshots before the crash, but some of them said no, contradicting their story. This is the reason he crashed. Then the other body over there was hit twice."

"With all the commotion, they may have misinterpreted what happened. It happens all the time, partner."

"Yeah, I guess you're right. Maybe I'm thinking into this too hard because of who is involved."

"We all are grieving right now. Who wouldn't, when a fellow officer is killed? All I can say is, that son of a bitch will get was coming to him."

"That is something we can both agree on." He sighed. "We'll get this guy Jered, I promise."

TEN

Word gets out fast when a cop is killed. The warehouse district was a media circus by the time Eric and Sonya were able to slip away. They left their captain to talk with the reporters because they wanted to check out a lead. After doing some calling around, one of the officers was able to find out that a pawn shop in town had the same kind of knife.

"This is the place," Sonya said, pulling over to the curb.

They walked into the shop, looking around at all the different styles of knives that were on display. The clerk was standing at the counter talking with a customer. They headed in his direction. Before they had the chance to pull their badges, they heard something crash in the back of the store. Someone was running. Eric drew his weapon and took flight behind the counter.

"Sonya, around the back."

She pivoted and ran out of the store, looking for a way into the alley. Eric moved through the back of the building quickly, gun aimed at the ready just in case whoever was trying to get away had a weapon of their own. He found the back door ajar and poked his head out. Sonya flashed by him, chasing after someone in black jeans, a black jacket, and a cap with the brim pulled down over their head.

Whoever it was, was a powerful runner, an athlete, certainly. They were carrying a black knapsack, but were still able to chew up ground, putting distance between the runner and Eric's partner. Eric spun around, raced back through the store, jumped into the car, and pulled off trying to cut the runner off. He came flying around the corner and caught a glimpse of the suspect as he dodged a pedestrian and vanished at the end of the block. It was astonishing how fast he had covered that distance. Sonya was only just coming out of the alley, at least a hundred yards behind the runner.

"That motherfucker is fast," Det. Morris

mumbled to himself.

Eric felt like flooring it and roaring after him, but he knew they were already beaten. He would have run into a dead end and wouldn't have been able to go any further. He turned the sirens off, stopped next to Sonya, and got out.

"You okay, partner?"

She was bent over, hands on her knees, drenched in sweat and gasping for air. Eric was laughing at her as she leaned on the car.

"Did you see that guy go?" she croaked. "Looked like the Flash or something."

"Impressive," he said. "Question is, who is he, and why the hell was he there?"

"Let's see if our pawnshop clerk can answer that," Sonya replied, getting in the passenger seat.

~ ~ ~

After nine and a half hours of interrogation, the pawn shop clerk gave up the name of the person that fled the scene, and an address where he may be hiding. This was probably the best break they would get in this case. Somehow all the murders, including the one of his friend captain Charles Ingram, were connected. Eric parked a couple of blocks away from Marlboro Road and waited for his SWAT team to arrive.

When the twelve-man team was finally in place, they breached the home using stun grenades. What they found in the kitchen would forever be embedded in their minds. Sonya ran out of the house and threw up on the curb. Samantha's head sat on the counter, and the rest of her body was sprawled out on the floor in a pool of blood. Det. Lee walked back into the room still looking flustered, but focused.

"You good?" Eric asked, with a smirk on his face. She gave him a sarcastic look, letting him know to back off.

"Detectives, you better come take a look at this," the SWAT commander said.

They followed him up the stairs, down the hall, and into a back room. A tripod was set up with a digital camera attached. The mattress was filled with so much blood, it looked like a massacre.

"Get a forensic team up here ASAP to sweep the area," Eric said, barking out orders to the officer standing close to him. "I want every inch of this place dusted for prints, and get me samples of this blood to the lab. I want to know who it belongs to by tomorrow."

"Looks like this was where she was killed. You think others were slaughtered up here too?" Det. Lee asked, looking around at all the blood splatter on the walls and floor.

"We'll know soon enough," he replied, looking through a trashcan that was sitting near the door.

Nothing was in there but a couple of cigarette butts. Eric took them out, placed them in a plastic evidence bag, and passed the bag to one of the CSI guys for processing. A cell phone rang while he was talking, causing him to look around. Eric followed the sound, leading outside the room and down the hall to another room.

"What is it?" Det. Lee asked, following behind

him.

The sound was getting louder as they got closer. When Eric walked into the other room, he could see the phone sitting on the window ledge. He slowly approached it, Sonya looking around for anything that may have looked out of place. It stopped and then started up again. The caller ID came up anonymous. Eric looked at Sonya, who was looking just as confused as he was.

"Answer it," she told him.

"Hello!" Silence! "Hello!"

"I knew you would eventually find my little playhouse," the distorted voice on the other end began. "Did you enjoy the little present I left you?"

Eric started waving his hand back and forth, telling Sonya to put a trace on the call. She quickly pulled out her cell and called it in.

"You want to tell me what all this is about? If you're such a tough guy, why don't we meet somewhere and talk face-to-face?" Eric kept looking at his partner, who was motioning for him to keep going. "Why did you kill a cop?"

"Don't patronize me, Detective. I know you're trying to trace this call. It won't work."

"What is it that you want?"

"You'll find out soon enough, or will you? The clock is ticking. I hope y'all enjoy the show. I hear it's a blast."

"What does that . . . ?" the call ended. Eric took a moment to decipher what the caller just said. Those last words stuck to him. "Everyone get out of the house now."

He pushed Sonya out of the room. They took flight heading for the nearest exit. You could hear the explosion as they reached the door, followed by another one. The blast knocked them out the door, onto the ground. Eric shielded his partner with his body from the flying debris. After the explosion, Sonya's ears were ringing so loud that she couldn't hear Eric talking to her.

"Sonya, Sonya, can you hear me?"

Sonya opened her eyes, trying to gather her wits.

Her vision was blurry, head was bleeding, and shoulder ached. Other than that, she was okay. She tried to stand up, but Eric wouldn't let her until she was treated by medical.

"I'm okay, really! What the hell just happened?" she asked, holding her head.

"This son of a bitch tried to fry our asses. You just relax while I help the other officers."

The detective rushed back into the burning building, trying to help any of the other trapped cops, but was unsuccessful. Five other cops were injured in the blast, two of them severely. All the evidence was on the verge of being destroyed because of the fire, including the decapitated body.

ELEVEN

A shley broke their kissing session, smiling at Tony. That brought him back into the present moment as he stared at her.

"Are you going to kiss my other lips?" she asked seductively.

He answered her by kissing her on the mouth before helping her out of the oversized T-shirt, revealing a work of art. Her body was beautifully toned from years of running track. Her nice pale complexion appeared smooth and flawless. She had nice full breasts with light brown areolas, and between her thick firm thighs was a perfect shaved mound. His favorite part of her body was her firm round butt.

He slowly and softly kissed her breasts, licking and sucking each one. He eased down further to her flat, slightly muscular stomach. Ashley released a sexy moan when he reached his destination, sticking his tongue inside her pussy. She arched her back and pushed forward as he used his tongue to spell out his name on her clitoris, while loving the taste of her body. It wasn't long before she pulled him up and gave him a passionate kiss.

"It's your turn, baby," she said, switching positions with him.

Once she was on top, she grabbed his erect penis with her right hand and brushed her long hair over her shoulder with her left. She looked up at him, showing her beautiful smile before inserting his manhood into her mouth. Tony closed his eyes as she did her thing, loving the feeling. She slowly sucked his penis from the base to the head, gently holding it between her teeth ever so softly while lightly grinding them back and forth over it. This drove him crazy. Ashley worked her way back up his body with kisses.

"Put it inside me," she whispered as she straddled him.

"Oh yeah, is this what you want with your naughty ass?" he said, grabbing his manhood and guiding it into her warm, wet love canal. The heat from her pussy almost made him cum instantly.

Ashley eased herself down, taking him all the way inside. She started to roll her hips as he palmed her ass with both hands, guiding her up and down. She moved his hands, pinning them down by his wrists.

"I'm running the show today."

She stared down at him as she made her vaginal muscles contract. Tony closed his eyes in ecstasy, enjoying the feeling of the beautiful woman. Moans escaped both of their mouths. Her grip around his wrist tightened when she felt her orgasm strongly working her way out.

"I'm cumming!"

Tony felt her body convulsing and took back over, breaking free from her grip, grabbing hold of her waist, and plunging in and out. Ashley loved and hated how deep he was going inside of her. It was the pain and pleasure that brought her to another orgasm.

"Damn, baby, you gotta have the best pussy in

the world," he grunted, feeling his own orgasm building up. He tried his best to hold back, but the way she was working her hips only confirmed that he was fighting a losing battle. "Here it comes." His load spilled deep inside her, and dripped out when his penis popped out from her vagina.

After a quick shower, Ashley walked out of the bathroom and took her damp towel off, dropping it to the floor. She grabbed a bottle of baby oil from her overnight bag, and poured a generous amount into her hands before rubbing it all over her gorgeous nude body. Once she was finished, she looked at her reflection in the mirror, running her hands through her long, flowing hair. Tony examined her figure, liking what he saw. Her stomach was flat, her breasts were high and perky, and her butt was round and firm just like it was four years ago when they worked together.

"You know your body hasn't changed one bit since the last time I saw you?" Tony said, sitting up.

"I still remember sneaking off to be with you,

leaving my husband home with the kids. Now look at me, doing it all over again," she replied, smiling.

"I don't know why you're still with him in the first place. He don't do shit for you."

"Two reasons: because when I married him, it was for better or worse, and we have a family together," Ashley responded, giving him attitude.

"But yet, you're here with me right now."

"Tony, don't start your bullshit. You're the one that said you didn't want commitment. I like what we have, so why can't we just enjoy it?"

"I'm cool with it. I guess we should be getting up out of here."

Tony went into the bathroom to take a quick shower. That quick shower ended up turning into another hot sex-a-thon when Ashley stepped in with him. After two more hours they were both dressed and heading out the door. Tony kissed Ashley, and she hopped in the awaiting Uber and headed home. Tony got into his car and pulled off, not paying any attention to the car pulling out behind him.

~ ~ ~

Sonya was relaxing in the tub watching the ten o'clock news, recovering from the injuries she suffered. They were talking about the large number of murders that had the city on edge. A couple of the reporters even blamed it on the police, saying they weren't doing enough to solve the case. Sonya was living proof that that was far from the truth. Her bruised face and fractured shoulder said it all.

She leaned back even further, enjoying the feeling from the jets. The tingling sensation between her legs caused her hand to ease down and slip in between her thighs. She gently stroked her clit in a circular motion, making it swell up. One, two, and three fingers entered her pussy.

Placing one leg on the edge of the tub gave her easy access to her love tunnel. She closed her eyes trying to please herself, but it wasn't working. She needed more, so she headed into the bedroom to retrieve her twelve-inch dildo that was hidden inside her panty drawer.

"You will have to do," she said, stroking the rubber toy up and down.

Sonya climbed onto her king-size bed, lifting her legs up to her buttocks. She stuck the dildo in her mouth, lubricating it, before rubbing it across her vagina. By this time she was soaked from the anticipation of being filled up with the thickness of her pleasure tool. She started off with the tip, slowly penetrating her, and inch by inch, she inserted the rest.

"Ohhh shiiiittt," she screamed out.

It felt so good that she had to switch positions. Sonya squatted down onto the rubber dick like she was sitting on top of the real thing. The whole time she was pleasing herself, she imagined it was her partner's dick she was riding. For some reason, Eric saving her life made her want to make love to him. This wasn't the first time she felt this way. It happened every time they risked their lives together.

Her pussy muscles wrapped around it, and the friction from the humping and the thought of it being

Eric had her squirting all over the bedsheets. She had forgotten all about the pain from her shoulder. When it was all said and done, she still wasn't fulfilled. Sonya wanted the real thing. She wanted Eric. Fed up with hiding her emotions, she snatched her cell phone off the night table and went through the names until she came to his. Just as she was about to hit the Send button, it started ringing. It was his picture and phone number showing on the screen. She hit the Accept button.

"You gonna live a long time. I was just thinking about you," she said, leaning back on the headboard.

"I hope it wasn't anything bad," he replied.

"No, I just need you to come over right now and fuck the shit out of me," she wanted to say, but didn't have the courage to. The sound of his voice had her juices flowing all over again. Instead she just changed the subject. "What's going on? Tell me you got something?"

"Not yet, still waiting on forensics to come back."

"So what's on your mind at 11:30 at night?" she asked, hoping he made the first move.

"I was just calling to make sure you were okay after the day we had, and see if you needed anything?"

"What I need I can't get over the phone," she mumbled.

"What you say, partner?"

"Um, I said I'm okay for now. I just took a shower, so I'm going to lie here with my Ben & Jerry's ice cream and catch a show or two before I call it a night."

They talked for about ten more minutes before ending the call. He told her that he would stop by in the morning and bring her breakfast before he went into work. Sonya took a couple aspirins and watched a repeat of Temptation Island until she fell asleep.

TWELVE

The funeral home was packed over capacity with family, friends, and law enforcement. There were over two hundred officers in attendance. They had all come out, not to mourn, but to celebrate the homecoming of Captain Ingram. His wife and two kids sat in the front row along with Eric, who was comforting the youngest one, Melanie. She was taking it the hardest out of the two because of how close they were. She was daddy's little girl.

Sonya sat behind them along with the mayor and commissioner. Outside looked like a media frenzy. There were reporters everywhere, trying to get inside. Chaplain Mary Wildes, his childhood friend, was the one who delivered the eulogy. By time she finished, the whole church was left in tears. Eric and five other pallbearers slowly carried the casket outside to the awaiting hearse. Once it was securely locked down, everyone got into their vehicles and waited for the police-escorted convoy.

"That was a beautiful eulogy she gave back there," Mrs. Ingram said, patting Eric on the leg. She stared out the window as they passed by her neighborhood.

"I couldn't have delivered it better myself. We will catch the person that did this, I promise," Eric replied. Deep down inside, this case was one of the hardest he ever encountered. There was someone out there killing random people, and he couldn't figure out how any of them were connected.

"I appreciate you being here. Jered use to talk so highly of you when he came home from work. You were like the son he never had."

Eric just nodded his head because he didn't know what to say. When they pulled into the cemetery, everyone unloaded from their vehicles and gathered around for the final benediction. The officers performed a twenty-one-gun salute as the trumpet played and they passed the flag to the family. In honor of the captain, Sonya sang "Amazing Grace."

Once the funeral was over and the casket was

lowered into the ground, everyone dispersed back to their vehicles. As Eric headed toward the family car with the Ingram family, he noticed a familiar face staring at him from a distance. It was Veronica.

"What is she doing here?" he mumbled to himself. "Excuse me for a moment."

"Is everything okay?" Mrs. Ingram asked, looking in the direction of the woman.

"Everything is fine. I will be right there. You just take the kids to the car."

He walked toward Veronica, who was standing near another gravesite. As he got closer, he was able to read the name that was engraved on the tombstone: Samantha Bennett. Her daughter was buried at the same cemetery as Jered, what a coincidence.

"Veronica, how are you doing?"

"I don't really know how to answer that question. I miss my baby so much."

"Sorry I didn't attend the funeral. As you can see, our killer has struck again," he said, pointing toward the gravesite of his mentor.

"Yeah, I've been watching the news. So what are you doing to put this asshole in the ground? I don't think he should be able to walk this earth breathing anymore, and I'm quite sure that all the other families that lost a loved one feel the same."

"That's not how the law works. Sure I would love nothing more than to unload my clip into his chest, but I can't do that. As an sworn officer, I have a duty to perform, and that's bringing this man to justice and letting the courts decide his fate."

"I'm sorry. It's just hard knowing that he's still out there and not knowing when he will strike again. It's hard to sleep, knowing he knows where I live. Who will be next? Will it be me, or will it be you or someone in your family?"

The thought of this maniac harming his niece or sister crossed his mind plenty of times. Hearing her say it only intensified his thoughts. As if she could hear his heart beating, she placed a hand on his chest.

"Just get him off the streets," she said with a sense of urgency in her voice.

"I will, that's a promise. Do you have anyone that will stay with you until I do?"

"My sister moved out here from Philly, so she will be here tomorrow."

"Great! I will check on you tonight and make sure you're okay. I'll stop by at around eight."

"I'll make dinner for you to show my appreciation, so come with an appetite."

"Thank you," he said, giving her a friendly hug, knowing that people may have been watching them talk. He headed back over to the limo.

Veronica was so excited about him coming over later that she rushed back to her car to head to the market for some groceries. She planned on making the meal herself.

"Who was that beautiful lady you were talking to?" Mrs. Ingram asked soon as he shut the door.

"One of the grieving victims," he replied before leaning his head back on the headrest.

~ ~ ~

When Eric arrived at Veronica's home, the aroma

of steak, baked macaroni and cheese, biscuits, and collard greens hit his nostrils. He got out of his vehicle and rang the doorbell. Less than a minute later, she answered the door wearing an apron with nothing under it but a cream-colored bra and panty set. Eric's eyes lit up with excitement.

"Wow, I thought I came to check up on you and eat dinner. I wasn't expecting this," he stated, staring at her backside as she walked away from the door.

He closed and locked the door behind him and followed her into the dining room where she had set up two plates of food.

"I gave the maid the night off so we could enjoy some alone time," Veronica said, looking over her shoulder and at the same time bending over the table to give him a perfect view of how her ass was swallowing up her thong. "What we do in that time is totally up to you. Which meal do you want first?"

"Hmmmm, let me think about that for a minute," he said, rubbing his beard with two fingers. "You definitely make a great argument."

"Don't take too long. Not only is the food getting cold, but so is this."

Veronica sat on the table, spreading her legs to give him a perfect view of her pussy lips poking through the fabric of her thong. She stuck a finger into her mouth, lubricating it, and pulled her thong to the side, sticking it inside. The whole time she was performing her sexual act, Eric stood there stroking his penis, making it come to life.

"I think my decision has been made. Let's see what your bedroom looks like." He smiled, lifting her from the table and carrying her up the stairs.

"Wise choice. Don't hold back either. We have all night."

When they entered the room, he playfully but gently tossed her onto the bed. She laughed and then stood up. The room had a dim, romantic glow from the moonlight entering through the open drapes. Eric stood there, watching Veronica as she slipped out of her shoes and the apron she was wearing. She motioned with her finger for him to come to her.

She put her hands on her hips, staring at his handsome face as he made his way to her. Veronica just loved seeing how shy he acted around her. When he finally made it within reach, she stroked his cheek and then pulled him closer and kissed him. The sexual tension was building by the second as she stuck her tongue down his throat. When she broke their embrace, Veronica rested her hand on his chest and felt his heart racing.

"You're not scared are you?" she teased, looking up at him.

He glanced down at her with a look as if to say, "Are you fucking serious?" Veronica immediately got the hint and started unbuttoning his shirt. Once she got it off, she gasped at the sight of his upper body. This was her first time seeing this part of him. She ran her hands over his shoulder and arms, feeling every cut and ripple of muscle.

"Nice!"

She traced his eight-pack physique with her index finger. Eric pulled off her Victoria's Secret bra, revealing her firm breasts with large dark nipples. Veronica quickly loosened his belt and unbuttoned his pants while ordering him to take his shoes off. After he removed them, she pulled off his jeans. Slowly, she went back up to his boxers and couldn't help becoming even hornier from looking at his bulge. She helped him out of them with a big-ass smile on her face, at the same time licking her lips in anticipation.

She stared at his erection, wanting to put it in her mouth, but knew it was too soon. She stood up and took off her thong, and all of a sudden, things changed. Eric started running his hands lightly over her entire body, sending what felt like an electrical charge through her. He cupped her breasts as he kissed her while rubbing his thumbs back and forth across her nipples. He sent her into the abyss of ecstasy. He stopped her long enough to turn her around and then started softly kissing the nape of her neck.

Veronica, who felt the warm flesh of his

manhood pressing against the cleft of her butt, pushed back on him as he continued to expertly manipulate her body with his hands. Eric ran his hands lightly over her stomach and then gripped it tightly. When he stuck it between her legs, she couldn't take it anymore.

"Oh my God, I need you inside of me," she moaned.

Veronica turned around and wrapped her arms around his neck before frantically kissing him. She pulled him down onto the bed with her as he kissed her neck before lightly biting down on her collarbone, which sent a tingle through her body. She reached between them and grabbed Eric's penis, guiding it inside her. She released a loud moan. Eric tried slow stroking her, but Veronica wasn't having any of that. She wanted it hard and fast. She grabbed his butt and started working him in and out of her. Eric began pounding her pussy with such a force that the bed frame broke.

"Opppps! I'll get that fixed tomorrow," Eric

said, still stroking away.

"Don't worry about it. I have a new one coming anyway," she moaned, feeling an orgasm coming. "Harder, faster, oooh I'm about to cum. That's it, baby, right there."

It didn't take too much longer for her to squirt her juices all over his dick. Two minutes later, Eric was releasing his own load inside of her. She squeezed her pussy muscles together, keeping him inside. It drove him crazy the way she was able to squeeze his semen out, without him doing anything. He went into the bathroom to wash up real quick. When he came out, Veronica was lying there with her head resting on the back of her hand, smiling.

"Now that we got the rough stuff out of the way, I want you to make love to me, daddy," she purred.

"Anything you want," he replied, hopping back into bed. He slowly entered her from the back, taking his time with each thrust.

She looked over her shoulders, letting him know that it felt so good. Eric was putting it down just the way she needed him to. There was so much emotion running through their bodies, that it made the sex just that much more intimate.

After a perfect balance of sensual lovemaking and hard sex, Veronica lay awake in Eric's arms as he slept peacefully. She still felt the buzz from the afterglow of their escapade. She kissed him on the lips, wondering if they could somehow be together after it was all said and done.

THIRTEEN

At nine that morning, Eric called into work to take a personal day. He wanted to take some time off to figure out why his city was being targeted. He put on his sweats and went for a jog. He studiously avoided looking at newspaper stands that would make him want to stop and read. The run gave him time to clear his head and get his mind right.

When he got back home, he took a nice hot shower and put on some clean clothes. He was about to cook some breakfast when his cell phone rang. Looking at the caller ID, he had a feeling it wasn't going to be good news. Still, he couldn't ignore it.

"Hello!"

"Hi, Eric. This is Larissa White. Would you hold for Commissioner Daly?"

Eric sat down at the kitchen table. He knew that calling in for a personal day after the chaos of the last few weeks might cause a few grumbles. But a call from the commissioner's office? What did he want with him?

"Eric?" Daly said.

"Hi, Commissioner," he said. "I can't tell you how sorry I am about what happened to your brother, or any of the other victims . . ."

Whenever the commissioner contacted you personally, something big was up. Eric had been on the bad end of getting his head rung by him before, but he had one of his high-ranking officers do it. He cut him off brusquely.

"We'll talk about that later. Right now we have a bigger situation to deal with, and as of now, you're being promoted to sergeant. Don't make me regret this."

A puzzled look came over Eric's face. He had never even thought about taking the test, and here he was being promoted by the PC. If anyone should have gotten the promotion, it should have been Sonya. She had been a detective longer.

"Sir, thanks but no thanks. My partner deserves that promotion more than I do. I can't do that to—"

"Calm down," the commissioner said, interrupting Eric once again. "She also has been promoted."

"Damn, seriously? I mean, thank you, sir."

"I didn't do it to fill up some empty spots; I did it because we needed to. You will still have to pass the test in order to officially be on paper. However, right now you and Sonya will be in charge of a new unit that we just assembled called Intelligence. You can pick your own team, but it needs to be done by the end of the week," the commissioner told him.

"What about our current cases? Aren't they priority right now?"

"Those cases are definitely priority. That's why I have authorized this unit. Meet with your captain to go over all the particulars and to switch your credentials. As of this moment, your Intelligence Unit will handle all sensitive cases. You will report only to the mayor, me, and your captain. Are we clear?"

"Crystal!" Eric replied, trying to hold back the excitement he was feeling.

All this had come days after he had fucked up a drop, gotten a woman's daughter killed, and still had a serial killer on the loose. After he got off the phone with the police commissioner, he started to called Sonya, but she was already calling him.

"I guess you just received the news too," she said as soon as he answered.

"Yes, I just got off the phone with the PC. So we're in charge of the Intelligence Unit, huh? How did this happen?"

"I'm not sure, but I think we need to celebrate tonight. How about we get a couple of drinks? I will be leaving here around seven."

"I'll meet you at the bar. Congratulations, partner," Eric replied before ending the call.

~ ~ ~

Later that night, instead of meeting up at the bar, they decided to eat at Applebee's. Sonya sat across from him, sipping on her apple martini and picking through the salad she was eating. Eric ate his steak and talked about how they would be handling all their cases. By time they left the restaurant, Sonya was a bit tipsy.

"I never seen you this way before," Eric told her, helping her into his car. "You're definitely not driving home tonight. You can just crash at my place."

"Good, because I wasn't going to make it home anyway," Sonya replied, punching him on the arm.

"Tomorrow we pick our team." He looked over at his partner, and she was knocked out. "I guess someone can't hold their liquor."

When they got back to Eric's crib, he helped Sonya to one of the rooms and laid her in the bed. He removed her shoes and placed a blanket over her. As soon as her face hit the pillow, she was out like a light. Eric shook his head as he walked out of the room smiling, closing the door behind him. He went into his room and started watching a Netflix movie.

About an hour later, Eric turned off the television and sat the remote on the nightstand. Then he went into the kitchen to get a bottle water. Sonya came out of the room yawning.

"Damn, I must have been tired. Thanks for letting me crash here, but I better get home. Can you take me back to my car?"

"You might as well wait until the morning," Eric said, passing her a water.

When their hands touched, she could feel the electricity flow from his body to hers. She moved away quickly, not wanting him to know there was a lot of sexual tension running through her. Too late! He already picked up on it, because he was feeling the same way. Maybe it was the few drinks he had at the restaurant, but Sonya was looking even more beautiful than she ever did. He was starting to wonder why she didn't have someone special in her life. He stepped closer to her.

"Do you think this is a mistake?" Sonya didn't answer. "I hope not."

His words were like some kind of incendiary device; her blood flamed. He leaned down and kissed her lips gently, sucking on her lower lip.

"I want to bite this lip," he murmured against her mouth and carefully tugged at it with his teeth. Sonya moaned, and he smiled.

"Mmmmmm," she moaned, closing her eyes.

"Please, Sonya, let me make love to you."

"Yes," she whispered, because that's what she'd been wanting him to do for quite some time now. His smile was triumphant as he released her and led her to his room.

His bed was enormous. Sonya was quaking like a leaf. This was it. Finally, after all this time, she was about to have sex with her partner. Her breath was shallow, and she couldn't take her eyes off him. He stepped out of his shoes and his pants. He opened the top drawer and pulled out a pack of condoms. Usually he would go in raw, but this time was different. This was his partner.

Eric strolled slowly toward her, confident, sexy, eyes blazing, and her heart began to pound. Her blood instantly started to pump through her body. Desire, thick and hot, formed in her belly. Eric stood in front of her, staring down into her brown eyes.

"Let's get this shirt off you," he said softly and lifted it over her head. He tossed it on the floor. "Do you have any idea how bad I want you right now?"

Sonya's breath hitched. She couldn't take her eyes off him as he ran his fingers down the side of her face and down to her laced bra. The muscles in the deepest, darkest part of her clenched in the most delicious fashion. Leaning down, he kissed her. His lips were demanding, firm, and slow, molding hers.

"Damn, partner, you have the most beautiful skin. I want to taste every single inch of it."

"Tonight we are not partners, just two adults exploring a new desire," she replied.

Eric put his arms around her and hauled her against his body, squeezing her tightly. One of his hands was massaging her D-cup breasts, while the other traveled down her spine to her waist and down to her butt. He squeezed it gently. The tighter he held her, the more Sonya could feel his erection, which he languidly pushed into her pelvic area. She moaned in his ear, causing him to get even more aroused.

Eric eased her toward the bed, until the back of her knees hit the frame. He dropped to his knees, grabbing her by the hips with both hands, ran his tongue around her navel, and nipped his way to her hipbone and across her belly to the other side.

"Ah," she groaned.

Eric reached up to undo the button on her jeans and pull down her zipper. Without taking his eyes off her, he moved his hands beneath the waistband, skimming her and moving to her ass. He wanted to take his time with Sonya, because it was their first time and she wasn't like the other women he fucked. His hands slid slowly down her backside to her thighs, removing her jeans in the process. He stopped and licked his lips, never breaking eye contact.

Eric leaned forward, running his nose up the apex between her thighs. Sonya could feel his nose touching the front of her pussy lips.

"You smell so good," he murmured, and closed his eyes. A look of pure pleasure was on his face, and

Sonya practically convulsed.

Without saying a word, he pushed her back onto the soft mattress. Still kneeling, he grabbed her foot and removed her socks one at a time. Sonya raised up on her elbow to see what he was doing. He lifted her foot by the heel and ran his thumbnail up her instep. It was almost painful, but she could feel the movement echoed in her groin. Not taking his eyes off of her, he ran his tongue along her instep again, and then his teeth. She lay back on the bed, moaning.

"Show me how you pleasure yourself," he whispered. She looked at him with a frown. She wanted him to fuck her, and right now. "I want to see you make yourself cum."

"I want you to do it for me," she replied.

Eric quickly pulled off his pants, and leaned down over her. Grasping each of her ankles, he jerked her legs apart and crawled on the bed between them. He leaned down and kissed the inside of her thigh, trailing kisses up, over the thin lacy material of her panties, causing her to squirm.

"Oh shit," Sonya mumbled.

He dipped his index finger into the cup of her bra and yanked it down, freeing her breasts, but the underwire and fabric of the cup forced it upward. His finger moved to her other breast and repeated the process. Her titties swelled, and her nipples hardened under his gaze. Sonya was trussed up by her own bra. Eric gently blew on one nipple as his hand moved to the other, flicking it with his thumb. Sonya's pussy instantly became so wet that her juices seeped through her panties. Her fingers clasped the sheets tightly. When his lips closed around her other nipple, she nearly came on herself.

"Let's see if I can make you have the best orgasm of your life," Eric said as his hand moved down her waist, to her hips, and then cupped her pussy.

His finger slipped through the fine lace and slowly circled around her clit. He could feel the warmth and wetness radiating from it.

"Damn, you're so fucking wet. I have to see how you feel inside."

He thrust his finger inside her, and she cried out. He did it again and again. He palmed her clitoris, and she groaned. He pushed inside again, harder and harder. Suddenly, he sat up and ripped her panties off, throwing them across the room. Pulling off his boxer briefs, his erection sprang free. Positioning himself between her legs, Eric grabbed one of the condoms, ripped it open, and pulled it over his ten-inch python.

"Pull your knees up," he ordered, and she was quick to comply.

Eric positioned the head of his erection at the entrance of her love tunnel. When he finally penetrated her walls, Sonya's body tensed up.

"Aargh!" she moaned as he pumped in and out at a steady pace. Then he stopped, letting her acclimatize to the intrusive, overwhelming feeling of him inside her.

Eric began to move at a slow pace inside of her and sped up in a relentless rhythm. Sonya met him thrust for thrust. Their bodies were in a synchronized rhythm.

"Cum for me, baby," he whispered.

At the sound of Eric's voice, Sonya unraveled, exploding with a powerful orgasm. Eric's pumps became faster and deeper when he felt his own orgasm coming. About forty-five seconds later, he shot his load into the condom. Sonya opened her eyes, and he had his forehead pressed against hers, his eyes still closed, his breathing ragged. Eric's eyes flickered open and gazed down at her. He was still inside her. Leaning down, he kissed her forehead before pulling out.

"I'd like to do that again," she whispered.

"Turn over."

When she turned over, he unhooked her bra and ran his hand down her back to her buttocks. He shifted so one of his legs pushed between hers, and he was half lying across her back. His hands moved down, skimming her waist, over her hip, and down her thigh to the back of her knee. Next he pushed her knee up higher, and her breath hitched. He shifted so that he was between her legs, pressed against her back, and his hand traveled up her thigh to her ass. He caressed her butt cheeks and trailed his fingers down between her legs.

"I have to fuck you from behind," he said, grabbing her hair at the nape in a fist and pulling it gently, holding her in place.

Eric's long fingers reached around her body and massaged her clitoris in a circular motion. Reflexively, her hips started to move, mirroring his hand, as excruciating pleasure spiked through her blood like adrenaline. Eric, without warning, inserted his right thumb inside her asshole, rotating it around, at the same time inserting two more fingers into her pussy. He simultaneously stroked the front wall of her vagina, and the walls of her ass.

"Fuck yeah, it feels so good," she screamed out.

Sonya closed her eyes, trying to keep her breathing under control, at the same time trying to absorb the disordered, chaotic sensation that his fingers were unleashing on her, fire coursing through her body. She let out another moan, pushing back on his fingers.

"You really get wet. Are you a squirter?" he joked.

"You'll find out eventually," she replied.

"Open your mouth," he commanded, thrusting his finger into her mouth. "I want you to taste yourself. Suck it, baby."

Sonya sucked on his fingers like they were a dick. It drove him crazy, watching how her tongue flicked across his finger. He needed his dick inside her again. This time without using a condom, he slowly eased back inside her already moist hole. It drove her insane the way he was teasing her with each slow thrust. The intermittent feeling of fullness was overwhelming.

"You feel so good," he groaned, feeling her insides start to quiver. She was about to cum again. "I want you to squirt all over me this time."

Her body went into convulse mode, and she began squirting all over his dick. It poured out like a faucet. Eric followed with two more sharp thrusts, and froze, shooting his load deep into her. He collapsed on top of her and realized what he had just done.

"Shit!" he mumbled under his breath.

FOURTEEN

The company party was in full swing in downtown Cleveland. There were about forty people there already, and more were scheduled to come. The guest of honor was moving through the crowd of people, shaking hands along the way. This was the day he was being promoted to senior vice president. Michael Turner had been with the company for a little over a year and already had passed over everyone in the company for the VP spot. It helped that his father was politically connected. The DJ played the music at a moderate volume so people could still converse without having to holler.

"Congratulations, Mike, even though you don't deserve it," a voice said, causing him to turn around. "What would people think if they knew you were a lying, cheating piece of shit?"

"That can only be one person," he replied, coming face-to-face with Elaine. She was standing there looking more beautiful than he remembered. "Why are you here?"

A year and a half ago Elaine and Michael were engaged to be married, until she found him in bed with another woman. He was once the love of her life. She had lost her virginity to him when she was eighteen, after their high school prom, and had been together ever since. He promised her that he would never do it again, and because she loved him, she stayed. He continued his cheating ways with multiple women over the next six months, including her best friend. The straw that finally broke the camel's back was when she went to his job for a surprise visit and found him in the back office getting head from his boss. Elaine had already come to the realization a long time ago that once a cheater, always a cheater, but that was crazy. He was receiving a blow job from a man. By time Michael got home that night, all his clothes were on the sidewalk.

"I was invited here by my friend. If I knew it was your party, I would have declined."

"Who is this friend?" Michael asked, looking around the room to see if he could pick him out.

"Why, so you can try to hit on him too? Well I have bad news for you, he doesn't like men, he loves pussy," she said loud enough that a few people walking past heard it and stopped trying to see what the commotion was about.

"You little bitch, you better watch your fucking mouth before I put something in it," he snapped, getting in her face.

"Looks like something was already in yours."

Michael was livid that she was trying to make a scene. This was his night. He raised his hand as if he was about to smack her. Before he had the chance to consider doing it, someone grabbed his arm. Michael turned in the direction of the person who had just touched him, and his facial expression quickly changed.

"You do that, and it will ruin everything you're trying to do."

Elaine couldn't believe who had just stopped him from making what could have been the worst decision of his life, because she had slipped her hand into her purse and gripped her switchblade tightly. She stood there speechless, and motionless. It was his old boss. The one she had caught him in the office with. They were still seeing each other after all this time.

"Yeah, you better listen to your man or whatever you want to call him. Do your friends even know that you're on the down low?"

By this time, Tony had heard Elaine yelling and made his way through the crowd. He walked over and stood beside her as she kept rambling on. The commotion had also caused a couple of security guards to make their way over. Noticing how much attention she was bringing to herself, Elaine calmed down.

"Come on, let's go enjoy the party before they make you leave," Tony whispered into her ear.

"I hope you die a horrible death. Someone needs to cut your little dick off and shove it up your ass," she yelled as Tony grabbed her by the hand and pulled her away.

The rest of the night went without another argument. Everyone enjoyed themselves by getting drunk and partying. Elaine didn't say anything, but in the back of her mind, she was still heated. He made it hard for her to find the perfect soulmate. Sometimes she even wondered if Tony could be the one.

~ ~ ~

Monday morning Michael sat in his office preparing for a meeting that was scheduled for 11:00 a.m. This was his first meeting as senior VP, and he wanted to stamp his imprint on the company. As he was finishing up, there was a knock and an envelope slid under the door. Michael got up and picked it up. He tore open the envelope and stared at the letter it held. His face looked puzzled.

"You will receive the makeover you always wanted, but only at the price of your own stupidity will it come," he said, reading the letter out loud. "What the hell is this crap?"

He quickly opened the door to see who had delivered the mail. There was only one person standing in the hallway, waiting for the elevator. Whoever it was was wearing a baseball cap and was dressed in a mailman uniform with their back to him.

"Hey, who sent this?" he asked, walking toward the mailman.

"Actually," the mailman said, pulling a silenced .45-caliber pistol from out of nowhere and turning and aiming it at Michael's heart, "I did."

When Michael saw who the mail service impostor was, his heart almost dropped to the floor. The impostor waited the split second it took for comprehension to dawn in the man's eyes. Before Michael could so much as blink, the impostor pulled the trigger twice. The sound was inconsequential, like someone clearing their throat. As Michael collapsed in a heap of dead flesh, the mail impostor sat the pistol down and pulled out a switchblade. Michael's pants were pulled down to his ankles, and with one swift motion, his penis sliced off his body.

The mail service impostor gripped up his gun, jumped in the elevator, and headed to the 1st floor. The lobby was crowded. Shielding the gun from sight, the impostor turned to the open doorway and scanned the scene outside. Seeing that the coast was clear, the imposter slipped out into the awaiting car in the alley and pulled off without being noticed.

~ ~ ~

Sonya rode in the passenger seat as Eric sped through traffic on their way to another crime scene. Neither said a word about the encounter they shared the other night, but knew they would have to talk about it eventually. The phone in Eric's pocket vibrated as he came to a stop sign. It was the chief of detectives calling.

"Where the hell are you, Morris?" His voice was forceful enough to burst a blood vessel.

"Moving as fast as I can, Chief," he replied. "I'll be there within five minutes."

"Well hurry up, this case has your name written all over it."

"Chief, what do you mean?"

"Maybe Trump finally went postal, and now he and Putin went on a crime spree together," the chief said sarcastically. "You and Lee were handpicked by the commissioner to run intelligence, so get your asses over here and figure it all out." The phone went dead.

"What'd he say?" Sonya asked when he put the phone down.

"Just that we need to hurry up," Eric replied, stomping down on the gas pedal, causing the Hemi engine to roar like a lion.

Downtown Cleveland looked like a police vehicle sales auction. There were cop motorcycles, Emergency Service Unit heavy rescue trucks, and dozens and dozens of officers all over the place. Sonya and Eric had seen hot crime scenes before, but this was way over the top. They badged their way past the yellow tape and headed inside the building. They were met by two plainclothes officers.

"Sergeant Morris, Sergeant Lee, right this way," Det. Pecko said.

"What can you tell us so far?" Sgt. Lee asked.

"All I can say, ma'am, is that it's a bloody mess. Somebody shot him in the heart and cut off his private parts. But that's not the worst part. Whoever did this, took his severed penis and stuck it up his ass. I guess they were trying to make a statement."

"What? Are you serious?" Sonya said, mouth wide.

"See for yourself," the other detective said as they stepped off the elevator.

The first person they ran into once they got off was the chief. He gave them a look as if to say, "It took you long enough." The body was lying in the hallway, right outside of his office, covered with a sheet. Eric walked over and pulled it back just enough to see the gruesome sight. Just like the young detective described, the victim's penis had been severed from his body and stuffed in his ass.

"Who found the body?" Eric asked, covering it back up and standing up. Det. Pecko pulled out his notepad to look at the notes he had taken.

"A Lucy McDougal. She is his new secretary.

Said she talked to him this morning and he said that he was coming in early to get ready for his first meeting. Friday night they had a party, honoring him for being promoted to senior vice president. Well when she arrived to assist him, this is how she found him."

"What about video?" Eric asked, looking at the multiple cameras on the walls.

"There's an officer in the security room with security going over the video. They think the person responsible for this had on a disguise, and also knew where the cameras were."

Sonya headed down to the security office to see what they had on tape, while Eric stayed with the Crime Scene Unit getting evidence. When she walked in, two security officers and a detective were looking over video footage.

"What did you learn?" she asked the detective.

"Whoever it was entered through the front door

sometime between 2:00 and 3:00 a.m., and left the same way."

"Wait, go back," Sonya said, noticing something. The security guard rewound the video. "Right there. Now, zoom in on that and freeze it."

The guard did everything he was instructed to do. They all watched as he moved the joystick around a few times and hit a couple of buttons.

"Make me a copy of that and give it to my detective and give me a printout of that photo. I want that DVD back to the tech lab ASAP."

"You got it, Sergeant," the detective replied.

Sonya headed back up to the crime scene to find out what else her partner had learned. Techs were still dusting the area for prints. Her stomach clenched like a fist when she saw one of the medical examiners loading the dead man's penis into a bag and placing it in a small cooler filled with ice.

"I had the techs take some prints from the

doorknob and the buttons from the elevator. If he touched it, we should be able to get a print," Eric said, watching them place the body in the body bag, load it onto the stretcher.

"Do we know what kind of gun it was that he was killed with?" Sonya asked one of the MEs as they passed them with the body in tow.

"The preliminary evidence says it was a small caliber like a .38 or .45 of some type, but once we dislodge the bullets from his body and get them to ballistics, we'll know for sure. Don't worry, you'll be the first to know once we know," the ME replied, continuing toward the elevator.

"Were you able to get anything from the video footage?" Eric said to his partner as they looked through the dead man's office.

"Enough to finally get this son of a bitch. I sent a picture to your phone and one to a media friend of mine to put on the air. Hopefully someone will recognize this person and come forward."

Just then, an officer rushed over to them, saying that there was a witness waiting downstairs that knew who murdered the victim. Sonya and Eric looked at each other and sprinted for the elevator.

FIFTEEN

Tony and Elaine lay in bed watching the season finale of Temptation Island. Elaine was getting horny just from rubbing on his chest. Ever since the party, she had been trying to spend more time with him, but it wasn't working like she thought it would. Even though he had been spending the night at her house, he still wanted his space. Elaine was willing to do whatever it took to keep him around, even if she had to be more aggressive.

After the show went off, Tony went into the bathroom to take a nice hot bath. As he was sitting down in the water, Elaine walked in with some clean towels and sat them on the towel rack.

"Why don't you join me?" he asked, rubbing the water over his body.

"If you insist," she giggled.

She stripped out of her nightgown and sat down

in front of him. The water felt so good as she leaned back into his chest. He placed his long legs over hers and pulled his feet apart, opening up her legs. He reached around her and played with her pussy. Elaine instantly braced herself for an explosive orgasm. It came within the next couple of minutes.

"Mmmmmm," she moaned as her body convulsed.

Tony's hands glided across her breasts, and she inhaled sharply as his fingers encircled them and started kneading gently, taking no prisoners. Her body bowed instinctively, pushing her breasts into his hands. She was supposed to be the aggressor, but yet it was the other way around. Her nipples were very tender from his less than delicate treatment. His growing erection pressed against her ass. He stopped and picked up the washcloth from the water. He poured some body wash on it and leaned down, washing between her legs. Elaine held her breath. His fingers were skillfully stimulating her through the cloth. Her hips started moving at their own rhythm, pushing against his hand. Sensation took over as her eyes rolled into the back of her head.

The pressure was building slowly, inexorably inside her. Another orgasm was mustering up all over again, and she was loving it.

"Feel it, baby," Tony whispered into her ear, very gently grazing her earlobe with his teeth. "Feel it for me." Her legs were pinioned by his to the side of the bath, holding her prisoner, giving him easy access to the most private part of her.

"Oh please," she moaned in somewhat of a whisper. She tried to stiffen her legs as her body went rigid. She was in a sexual thrall to this man, and he didn't let her move.

"I just cleaned you up. Now it's your turn to clean me," he murmured, stopping abruptly.

"What . . . oh my . . . but . . . I was . . . that's not

fair," Elaine was able to get out.

"Life's not fair either. Turn around."

When she turned around to face him, she was shocked to find he had his erection firmly in his grasp. Her mouth dropped open. It was so big and still growing from each stroke. She couldn't believe that all of that had been inside of her on numerous occasions. Elaine glanced up at him with a wicked grin on her face. She reached for the body wash, squirting some onto her hand. Never taking her eyes off of him, she parted her lips to accommodate her breathing, deliberately hitting her bottom lip and then running her tongue across it, tracing where her teeth had been.

Tony's eyes were serious and dark, and they widened as her tongue skimmed her lower lip. She reached forward and placed one of her hands around him, mirroring how he was holding himself. His eyes closed briefly. He moved his hand as hers took over.

Elaine moved her hand up and down along his shaft. Tony flexed his hips slightly into her hand, and reflexively she gripped him tighter. A low groan escaped from deep within his throat. His mouth dropped open as his breathing increased. Elaine leaned forward while he still had his eyes closed, and placed her lips around him and tentatively sucked, running her tongue over the tip of his penis.

"Fuuucck yeah," he groaned, opening his eyes for a brief second before closing them again.

Moving down, Elaine pushed him into her mouth. He groaned again. She twirled her tongue around the tip, and he flexed and raised his hips. His eyes were open now, blistering with heat. His teeth clenched together, and she pushed him deeper into her mouth, supporting herself on his thighs. She felt his legs tense beneath her hands. Tony reached up, grabbing her hair, and started to really move.

"Oh . . . baby . . . that feels good," he murmured.

Elaine sucked harder, flicking her tongue across the head of his impressive erection. Wrapping her teeth behind her lips, she clamped her mouth around him. His breath hissed between his teeth, and he groaned.

"Jesus. How far can you go? he whispered.

She pulled him deeper into her mouth so she could feel him at the back of her throat and then to the front again. Her tongue swirled around the end. Tony was her very own lollipop. She sucked harder and harder, pushing him deeper and deeper, swirling her tongue around and around. She was used to giving head, but she had no idea it would be such a turn on, watching him writhe subtly with carnal longing.

"Damn, I'm going to cum in your mouth," his breathy tone warned. He thrust his hips again, his eyes wide, wary, and filled with salacious need for her.

Tony's hands were really gripping her hair tightly. She pushed even harder, and in a movement of extraordinary confidence, she bared her teeth. It tipped him over the edge. He cried out and stilled, and she could feel warm, salty liquid oozing down her throat. Elaine swallowed quickly. His breathing was ragged as he opened his eyes and glared at her.

"Damn, don't you have a gag reflex?" he asked, astonished. "Shit . . . baby . . . that was . . . good, really good. That might be the best head I ever had in my life. You know you never cease to amaze me. I'm just wondering what got into you tonight? You're a bit frisky."

"What the hell is going on here?" Tony yelled, fixing his towel. Elaine did the same trying to cover up her goodies.

"We'll talk at the station," Eric replied.

SWAT finished clearing the rest of the house before Eric had a couple of officers retrieve some clothes for them to throw on. Once dressed, they both were handcuffed and thrown in the back of two different squad cars and hauled off to the station.

"Search this place for weapons, and I want to know the moment you find something," Sonya ordered the rest of the officers.

"You got it, Sarge."

"Let's get back to the station and see if we can get a confession," Eric stated, giving his partner a high five.

As they walked out of the home, they were greeted with all kinds of news cameras and reporters. Leading the pack was Sarah and her crew.

"Sergeant Morris, is it true that you have arrested the person behind all those murders?"

They were shooting all kinds of questions his way, hoping to get the answers. Eric only gave them a brief inquiry of the situation until he had all the facts.

"All I can tell you at this moment is that we have a person of interest. I can't tell you anything else until our investigation is thoroughly conducted. Thank you, that is all for now," Eric said, walking away.

As they pulled off, reporters kept snapping shots, while other cameras kept videotaping the scene. Sarah thought he would at least give her something more, but he didn't even so much acknowledge her. She needed to know what was going on with her boss, and the answer to her question just left.

SIXTEEN

"So how do you want to handle this? Good cop, bad cop? Or should we just get straight to it?" Sonya asked as they looked through the double glass mirror.

Elaine was sitting in the interrogation room with her head face down on the table. She had been sitting there for over two hours. In the other room, Tony sat patiently without a care in the world, wondering why he was there. Why did they storm into Elaine's house like that? Was she living a double life of some kind? These were some of the thoughts going through his head.

"I want to call my lawyer now," he yelled out, knowing they were listening.

"Let's go," Eric said, heading for the door. Sonya followed behind carrying a folder.

"My name is Sergeant Morris, and this is

Sergeant Lee."

"I don't give a damn who you are. I haven't done anything wrong, so why the hell am I here?" Tony snapped, banging his hand on the table.

"You need to calm down and we'll try to get to the bottom of this quickly, and maybe you can be home before daylight."

Sonya slammed the folder down and opened it up. She placed picture after picture on the table, spreading them out so that he could see them all. One look at the photos, and he knew what they were insinuating. His mouth dropped open at the horrific sight.

"I had nothing to do with this. Why are you showing me this?" he asked.

"We think your girlfriend may be involved with murdering all these people," Sonya began.

"That is not my girlfriend. She is just someone I have been seeing from time to time. You still haven't told me what it has to do with me."

"We're trying to build a timeline of events, and we're hoping you can help us out, Mr. McAndrew," Eric chimed in. "Do you or Ms. Frasier have an alibi for the following times and dates?" He began reading off a bunch of times, and Tony just sat there staring.

"I told you before, I want to call my lawyer. I'm not saying another word."

Seeing that they weren't getting anywhere with Tony, they decided to question Elaine. Eric let Sonya handle this one, but he was watching on the other side of the glass. When she stepped into the room, Elaine had this worried look on her face which played in Sonya's favor. That was the face of a person hiding something. She pulled up a chair on the other side of the table and sat down.

"Ms. Frasier, I'm not going to sit here and play around with all the dumb-ass questions," she started off saying. "You were at a party Friday and got into an argument with this man right here."

Sonya pulled out a picture of the deceased Michael Turner and placed it in front of Elaine. She looked down at it, her facial expression staying the same, and looked back up at the detectives.

"Yes, I was there. It looks like he finally got what he deserves if you ask me." She smirked.

Sonya kept a straight face hoping she would talk herself right into a confession. That's what most people that are guilty usually do.

"Elaine, all I want to know is, how do you know this man, and what was the argument about?"

"We were never arguing. I told him he was a booty bandit and that I hoped someone cut his little dick off," she said, holding up her thumb and pointer finger close to each other. "And shoves it up his ass. That is all I said to him. Then me and Tony finished enjoying the party."

"So security and another man didn't come over

and break up y'all's heated conversation?"

"They came over, but we were only talking. Maybe I was a bit loud. How would you feel if the man you were once engaged to was caught creeping with another man who just so happened to be his boss?" Sonya didn't respond. "You can accuse me of many things, but murder is not one of them."

"What about these other victims?" Det. Lee asked, spreading the rest of the pictures out on the desk.

"Who are they?" she replied, looking at the gruesome pictures. "I hope you're not accusing me of that. I'm a very successful reporter in this damn city. Matter of fact, I'm leaving." Elaine tried to get up.

"Sit your ass back down in that chair," Sonya ordered. "You're going to tell me why you killed these innocent people."

"I didn't kill anyone. Go to hell."

"Well you're going to tell me where you were during the time of these murders. Once we check out your alibi, then and only then will you be able to leave."

Eric was smiling from the other side as he watched his partner. His lust for her was growing stronger by the minute. He didn't know why he wanted her so bad right now. His thoughts were interrupted by Sarah as she came bursting through the door with a lawyer right behind her.

"I'm Joey Savino, and that is my client that you're interrogating without my presence. You people are violating her rights."

"What do you mean, you people?" Eric snapped back, feeling like he was racially profiling them because he was African American, and Sonya was mixed with Asian and black.

"Whoa, whoa, let's not jump to conclusions. I'm referring to you cops," he said in his own defense.

"You guys have some nerve, questioning my client without her lawyer. Is this how you get all your confessions?"

"First off, don't come into my station with that bullshit. She has yet to ask for a lawyer, which brings me to the question of how you knew she was here."

The whole time he talked, his eyes were on Sarah. She had seen that look before back when they met at the first news conference. The only difference was, this time it wasn't a lustful look.

"I called him," Sarah said.

"Let me speak to you outside," Eric said, motioning her toward the door. She followed him out.

"That's my boss you have in there, Eric. What did you think I was supposed to do when I saw you arresting her and Tony?" she asked, turning to him.

"I expected you to let me do my damn job and find out who is responsible for the death of all these innocent people. Sarah, I hate to say this, but your boss is a serial killer and needs to be stopped."

"We don't know that yet. You're passing judgment a bit too soon, don't you think?" Sarah told him.

"Sarah, listen to me, we have an eyewitness that places her at the party, saying what she wanted done to him. Not even three days later, he's dead, and the same exact way that she said. Coincidence, I think not," he said, looking at her angrily.

Joey opened the door and walked out. Eric could see from his demeanor that he was getting impatient with this whole situation. He walked right past them, heading for the interrogation room. Eric followed behind him as he busted in the room, interrupting Sgt. Lee.

"If you are not going to charge my client, we are leaving," he stated, grabbing Elaine by the arm, helping her out of the chair.

They were making their way toward the door, when Eric blocked them. From the look on his face, Joey assumed they weren't going anywhere.

"We have up to seventy-two hours to hold your client, and we're going to exercise that right, counselor," Eric said.

At that moment, district attorney Cynthia Young and ADA Kevin Bachman walked into the room. Cynthia had a confident look on her face that made Eric and Sonya look at each other. Whenever you got both of them in the same room, someone was going down. Before anyone said anything, Sonya was already slapping the platinum bracelets on Elaine.

"You have the right to remain silent. Any and everything you say can and will be used—"

"Stop and release her," ADA Bachman replied, cutting her off. Everyone looked dumbfounded. "She is not our suspect."

"What you mean? We have a witness," Sonya

said, reluctantly removing the cuffs.

"We found one of the murder weapons, and the DNA results came back matching someone else," Cynthia chimed in.

"Who?" Eric asked with a puzzled expression on his face.

"Tony McAndrew?" ADA Bachman replied. "Arrest him now."

Sonya and Eric rushed out of the room to catch up with Tony. They had just released him after thinking they had the person they wanted. When they stepped outside, he was about to get into a cab. Sonya was the first to grab him, followed by Eric. He was immediately handcuffed and taken into custody without a struggle.

"Why are you doing this? I didn't do anything," he yelled as they placed him in a cell. "It wasn't me, Detectives, it wasn't me."

SEVENTEEN

The courtroom was packed to capacity with officers, reporters, and family and friends of the victims as they waited for the judge to come out. This was Tony McAndrew's first arraignment hearing. The prosecution was going to seek the death penalty, which meant that today they would be asking the judge to remand him until trial. Eric and Sonya had just walked through the doors when the bailiff stood up.

"All rise, the honorable judge Walter Payne residing," the court officer shouted.

Everyone stood up out of respect for the judge as he walked out of the back room. He was in his late fifties but looked about forty and was physically fit. He sat down, adjusting his glasses and fixing his robe.

"You may be seated," he said respectfully.

"Your Honor, this is case number 19-73642, the State of Ohio versus Tony McAndrew." The bailiff passed him the folder.

"How does the defendant plead?"

"Brittany Sanchez for the defense," his attorney replied, standing up. "We plead not guilty, Your Honor."

"Let it go on record that the defendant has pleaded not guilty. How does prosecution feel about bail?"

"Your Honor, the State asks for remand until trial. The defendant is considered a flight risk and has ties in various other cities, along with the resources to relocate," ADA Bachman stated, causing Brittany to quickly intervene.

"My client is not a flight risk and is anxious to get these bogus charges exonerated and his name back in good standings. We're not asking for ROR. We would just like a reasonable bail, Your Honor."

The judge started taking his time looking over the file in front of him. It took him about three minutes before he reached his decision.

"Due to the severity of this case and the evidence

placed in front of me. It is in the best interest that you be remanded to the county prison until your trial."

"Your Honor, we ask that a suppression hearing be scheduled immediately," Brittany demanded.

"It is duly noted. I will get back to you on that," he replied, closing the folder. "Next case!"

Two sheriffs grabbed Tony by the arm and escorted him out of the courtroom. Elaine and Sarah sat in the back during the whole proceedings and couldn't believe how easily the judge had ruled in the prosecution's favor. However, they did understand how serious it was. Elaine saw Eric and Sonya leaving and ran out to confront them. Sarah followed thinking she was about to ask them some questions.

"This is all your fault," she said to the detectives. They stopped and turned around. "How can you sleep at night knowing that you falsely accused someone of murder?"

"Elaine, stop trying to take the side of that man. You know that he got what he deserves. You're lucky we caught him when we did, or you could have been the next one on his list," Sonya snapped.

"Fuck you," she replied, getting up in Sonya's face. Sarah quickly stepped in.

"Come on, Elaine. This is not the time for this. Besides, we have a story to get out before five o'clock."

"I hope you're happy now. You put a good man in prison," Elaine said as they walked away, leaving the detectives with confused looks on their faces.

~ ~ ~

"Hey, you! What are you doing here?"

"I came over to celebrate with you. We finally got your daughter's killer off the street," Eric said, holding up a bottle of Hennessey. He was standing in Veronica's doorway. "Are you going to invite me in?"

Sonya stepped to the side, allowing him access. Eric walked over and sat the bottle of liquor down on the table. There were two half-eaten plates of food sitting next to the sink.

"Did I come at a bad time?" he asked, staring at

the plates.

"No, me and my sister just got finished eating dinner."

Hearing that made Eric sigh with relief. He had forgotten that her sister had come to stay for a while. Eric put his hand under her chin and tilted her head back, giving her a peck on the lips. He had planned on spending the night at Sonya's, but when he got there, she was getting into another man's car. That's when he decided to see if Veronica was free.

"Where is she? I would like to meet her."

"She's out back taking the trash out." Just then, her sister walked through the door. "Here she is now. Eric, this is my sister, Ashley."

One look and Eric immediately noticed the resemblance. They could have passed for twins. The only thing that separated the two was Veronica's breasts were two sizes bigger and Ashley had auburn hair. Eric was staring too long, causing Ashley to speak.

"Take a picture, it will last longer," she joked,

sticking out her hand. "It's nice to meet you, Eric."

"Nice meeting you too!"

He shook her hand and felt her finger tickling his palm, before releasing it. After the introductions, the three of them sat down and had drinks. Veronica pulled out a few photo albums, showing Eric pictures of them growing up and baby pictures of Samantha. An hour later, Veronica and Eric went up to her bedroom.

Soon as they made it inside the room, they were all over each other. Neither bothered to even close the door. He kissed her passionately, forcing her lips apart with his tongue. The blood in her body started heating up immediately as she returned his kiss with her own passion. Eric's fingers reached inside the waist of her sweatpants and pulled them down to her ankles. Veronica stepped out of them one foot at a time and kicked them away. Her shirt came off next.

"No bra, I like that," he said, his hands reaching up and cupping her breasts. Her nipples puckered at his touch.

He turned her around and pulled on her nipples with his fingers. She groaned as the sensation flowed all the way to her pussy.

"You want me to make you cum this way?" he whispered.

"Mmmmm," was all she could say.

He continued the slow, sensuous torture, pulling gently. He pinched them, and her body writhed convulsively against him. Veronica gasped at the exquisite, acute pleasure and pain. He turned her around and could feel himself up against her ass.

"I don't think you're ready to cum yet," he said, stilling his hands and biting down on her earlobe and tugging at it with his teeth.

"Please," she moaned a little too loud.

Ashley was walking toward her room when she heard them. She slowly walked over to the opened door and peeked inside. Their backs were to her, but she knew what they were doing. She watched on, rubbing on her breasts. She wished she could call Tony, who she was just with a few days ago, but he was in prison, charged with murder. Her hands would have to do for now.

Eric's fingers hooked into Veronica's panties at the back, stretching them, and he pushed his thumbs through the material, shredding them and tossing them in front of her so she could see. His hands moved down to her vagina, and from behind, he slowly inserted his finger.

"Oh yeah, I see you are ready." He whirled her around so she was facing him. He put his finger in his mouth. "You taste so good."

At the time he turned Veronica around, Ashley ducked back behind the door. She scooted down and peeked back around to finish watching. Her sister started ripping off Eric's clothes. He took one of her hands and placed it on his erection. Catching on, she began stroking away, causing it to grow more and more with each touch.

"That feels so fucking good," Eric moaned.

Veronica pushed him onto the bed. He laughed as he fell on his back. She crawled up on the bed and sat astride him, rubbing his balls. His skin was so smooth . . . and hard. She leaned forward, her hair falling down the side of her face, and took him into her mouth.

"Jeez, baby," he groaned.

By now, Ashley had stood back up to get a better look at the action and had one hand down her panties, massaging her clit. The size of his dick had her drenched. Her eyes were closed as she stuck one and two fingers inside herself. Her moaning got louder as she moved in and out.

"Why don't you come join us?" a voice whispered. Ashley's eyes popped open nervously. Veronica was standing in the doorway smiling. She held out her hand. "Come on!"

This wasn't the first time they had a threesome with some lucky man. Actually, this would be their third time sharing one. Eric was shocked at first when he saw her come in. After the initial shock had subsided, he was excited. Both women climbed onto the bed, opposite sides of Eric. Veronica started massaging his balls again, while Ashley took him in her mouth, trying to deep throat all of him.

It was such an exhilarating feeling for them, teasing and testing him with their hands and mouths. Eric tensed underneath Ashley as she began running her mouth up and down his length, pushing him to the back of her throat. Veronica bent over, placing his balls in her mouth, sucking on them at the same time her sister was sucking his penis. The two of them were like pros together.

"Stop, I don't want to cum yet," he moaned trying to push them off, but they had firm grips on him. He wasn't going anywhere. "I need to get inside one of you now. The other can sit on my face."

Ashley was the first to straddle him. Veronica positioned herself right above his face, slowly lowering her body on to his awaiting tongue. Eric grabbed Ashley's waist with one hand, lifting her, and with the other he positioned her onto his throbbing dick. She groaned as he stretched her open. Her mouth hung open in surprise at the sweet, sublime, agonizing feeling.

"Oh shit, you're too big," Ashley murmured, placing her hands on his chest to stop him from pushing all the way in. "You're tearing my insides. Oh shhhiiiit."

"This is what she was imagining, so give it to her," Veronica moaned, grinding her pussy on his face. "All of it."

Eric flexed and swiveled his hips in the same motion, causing Ashley to groan. The sensation was radiating throughout her belly. Getting into the groove of things, she started riding up and down like Eric was a horse and she was the jockey. She clasped his hands, holding on for dear life. Veronica felt her orgasm building up and started sucking on Ashley's titties, at the same time sticking a finger into her pussy to go along with Eric's dick. About thirty seconds later, Veronica was squirting into his mouth. Eric swallowed everything. She moved off of his face and kissed her sister.

Eric's eyes were burning with wild anticipation.

His breathing was ragged, matching Ashley's as he lifted his pelvis every time she came down, bouncing her back up. With Veronica now watching, he grabbed Ashley's waist and picked up the pace. Up, down . . . over and over . . . It was feeling so good for both of them. The steady pounding pushed him over the edge. He came all inside her.

Ashley was right behind him, shouting incoherently and shooting her load all over his abdominal area. Both of their fluids spilled out of Ashley and onto the sheets. She collapsed on to his chest, overwhelmed by how he just ripped her insides apart. Even though it hurt, she wanted more.

"Whoa, that was breathtakingly awesome," Ashley said, catching her breath.

Eric tried to get up, but they pushed him back down.

"We're not done with you yet. Let me help you with this." Veronica smiled, grabbing his semi-erection and placing it into her mouth, getting him ready for round two.

EIGHTEEN

S herry was drying her hands with a dish towel when the doorbell rang. She assumed it was the delivery that her husband had been waiting for. She turned the stove on low so the noodles she was cooking didn't boil over, and went to answer it.

"Bachman residence, I presume," the stranger asked, pressing the snub-nosed barrel of the semi-automatic machine gun to the tip of her nose.

"Yes, can I help you?" she replied, her towel fluttering to the floor as she stared at the weapon nervously. She couldn't move an inch. She even almost pissed on herself from being so scared. "What do you want?"

"Aren't you going to invite me in, Ms. Bachman?" he said. Reluctantly, she stepped back. There was nothing she could do. She was worried about her two kids. The stranger smiled. "Thank you!"

When they walked into the kitchen, the two kids

were sitting at the table. The stranger lowered the weapon, hiding it out of sight of the children. They watched with mild curiosity. At their age, the sudden appearance of a stranger was just one of the many mysterious things running through their little minds.

"Hey, who are you?" the oldest one asked, sliding out of her chair.

Sherry swallowed, fighting the urge to dive across the kitchen and scoop her up out of harm's way. Instead, she just stepped forward to intercept Nicole and caught her hand.

"I'm one of your daddy's friends," the stranger said.

"I'm Nicole. Are you a lawyer too? Why are you dressed like that? What's behind your back?" She was asking question after question, not giving anyone a chance to respond. Her little brother giggled.

"Get rid of them before I get pissed off," the

stranger whispered, tapping Sherry on the arm.

"Go watch the movie in my room, now," she ordered.

"But I thought you said we couldn't watch TV in your room without you?" Nicole said.

"It'll be okay this one time, Nicole. Take your brother up there now, and stop mouthing back."

Nicole grabbed her brother's hand and scurried away, finally frightened by her mother's harsh tone. The stranger waited until they were out of sight before brandishing the gun and aiming it at her again.

"Get on the phone and tell your husband he needs to get home fast. You won't be lying if you say it's a family emergency."

~ ~ ~

"Cross reference that with all the information we got from the FBI's database. In order for this to be an open-and-shut case, we need to make sure we have exonerated all of our resources," ADA Cynthia said to her workers. They had been in the office all morning and afternoon, working on the McAndrew case.

With only a few days left before the suppression hearing, Kevin needed to make sure Tony was kept in prison and didn't get off on some stupid technicality. There was a lot riding on this case, and he didn't want to let any of the victims' families down. From the evidence they recovered from his home and the prints, this should be an open-and-shut case. Tony continued to deny that he had anything to do with it. All the times the murders were committed, his alibi couldn't be confirmed because he was home alone. That alone made him an instant suspect.

"The video surveillance across the street from his home shows him leaving his home around the time this murder occurred," Kevin stated, looking at the screen.

"Do we have any video of where he went?"

"Still waiting for the detectives to get back to me. However, none of the crime scenes had cameras at or around the immediate area, which is unusually strange, considering how technology is in this day and age."

"I totally agree with you. Check and see if maybe there were cameras but they weren't working," Cynthia stated, leaving the office.

Kevin sat down and started reading through all the files. He was wondering how the killer picked his targets, which was still a mystery, since he wasn't talking. His cell phone started vibrating on his desk.

"Hey, sorry, I'm going to be at work a little longer tonight," he said, answering his wife's call.

"I need you to come home. Nicole is not feeling too good. She has a temperature of 100, and she can't stop vomiting. I don't know if I should take her to the hospital or not."

"Okay, I'll just bring my work home and do it

there. Just put some ice on her forehead."

When Kevin ended the call, he gathered all the paperwork that he may have needed and headed out to get home in case he had to go to the hospital with his daughter. Outside the cold air felt good as he hit the alarm button on his car. As he drove home, he went back to brainstorming. Why did he kill captain Jered Charles Ingram, Samantha Bennett, or any of the other victims? What was the connection? He had a reason for what he was doing.

Instantly, the word psycho came to mind, but he was organized, smart, and very much in control all the way up until now. The way he was taking people out, he seemed more like Jason from Friday the 13th. What made him slip up all of a sudden? How did he know all of them? Kevin decided that he better look into their backgrounds also.

Kevin pulled into his driveway and stepped out of the car, carrying his briefcase. When he stepped inside the house, everything seemed quiet. He could see the flickering blue light coming from the television in the living room, which meant that the kids were still up. Since they couldn't have a TV in their rooms, they would watch the one in the living room. It was too late for them to be up anyway on a school night, or maybe his wife just wanted to keep her near until he got home. Kevin didn't hear any coughing or retching sounds as he got closer to the room.

"Hey, I'm home," Kevin yelled out.

When he first stepped into the living room, he could see the kids sitting on the couch half asleep. What really caught his attention was Sherry sitting on the other chair staring at him urgently.

"Why is everybody still up? Do we need to take her to the doctor or what?"

"No, it's time to have a seat with the rest of your family," said a voice from behind. The light flicked on.

That's when he spotted the lamp cord that bound Sherry's arms to the chair she was sitting in. It felt like his heart stopped. He was wondering what the hell was going on.

"I'll say it once more. Have a seat, or one of your kids will pay the price," the voice said. "I suggest you heed my words. You know exactly what I'm capable of."

Kevin turned around to come face-to-face with the angel of death. He couldn't believe who he was staring at. The killer was holding the gun tightly, and it was pointed steadily at his heart. Kevin sat down next to his kids, who still looked drowsy. He could tell that they had been given something to put them to sleep.

"What have you given my kids?" Kevin asked, checking their eyes. Both of their pupils were dilated. They couldn't even talk.

"They'll be okay. However, whether they live or die is totally up to you."

"What do you want? I don't have any money here, but I can transfer some to you if you give me an account number," Kevin said, trying to figure out a way to get his family out of harm's way.

"I don't want your money or any other materialistic items you may have to offer. You see, Mr. ADA Bachman, you are about to be a sacrifice for the greater good. First things first, I need you to go sit next to your wife."

At first, Kevin was reluctant to move, but all that changed when the intruder aimed the gun at the head of his younger child. They were so drugged up, they didn't have the slightest clue what was about to happen to them. Kevin stood and walked toward his wife.

"What now?" asked Kevin as he stood next to his wife.

The intruder directed him to sit down in the chair next to her, which he did. Once he was seated, his hands and feet were tied up with another cord. All of their mouths were duct-taped except for Kevin's.

"Now, don't do anything silly," the intruder said in a condescending tone. "I'll be listening, and if I hear something I don't like, you'll make me put a bullet in one of your kids' heads."

Kevin could see his wife cringe at the thought of something happening to their children. That was just the kind of thing he didn't need to hear right now, knowing that there was a chance of his kids being harmed. He watched as the intruder pulled out a black case from somewhere and opened it up on the floor. When Kevin saw what was there, he really got nervous.

"Listen, do whatever you want to me, but please leave my kids and wife out of this. I'm begging you," Kevin said as calmly as possible. "Do you hear me, motherfucker?"

Without saying a word, the intruder walked up to Kevin's younger kid and shot him at point-blank range in the head. The sound of the gun was muffled by the suppressor that was screwed on the tip. His wife tried to scream when she saw her son's brains hanging out of his head. Kevin puked all over his clothes.

"I need you to understand that I'm not playing. Counselor, I told you not to do anything silly. Well that also means talking out the side of your neck," the killer said with a blink stare. "Everything that happens now, is for a reason. This is all for the greater good."

"I'm a kill you," Kevin screamed, trying to break out of the restraints. His wrist was bleeding from him twisting and turning, trying to pop the cord.

"I see you need more convincing," the killer stated, grabbing a medical knife from the black case.

"This time, I'll make it as painless as possible."

"Kill me! Don't hurt my family. Please," Kevin pleaded one more time.

Nothing could prepare Kevin for what happened next. He watched as the killer stood over his wife, yanked her head back, and plunged the knife into her left eye, turning it until her eyeball popped out of its socket. She went into shock from the pain. The killer did the same thing to her other eye, before cutting off her ears and nose.

"Noooooo, stop it! Stop it!" Kevin said, crying. The tears were flowing freely down his face. Watching his wife being tortured was like it being done to him. "Please, what do you want from me?"

"I already have what I want. You! How do you prosecutors think you can just get away with putting innocent people behind bars? Do you even know how that impacts their families? I want to show you how it feels."

"Don't hurt anyone else. Just let my daughter go. This is between me and you," Kevin said calmly.

"Actually," the killer said with a sardonic smirk. "This thing is between me and whoever I say it's between."

Kevin kept trying to break free from the cord, but couldn't as he watched the killer walk over to his oldest daughter. She was still lying on the couch in a daze. He could tell that she had no clue what was going on around her. The killer pulled out a needle and poked it into the young girl's arm. Seconds later, her body went all the way limp.

"Don't worry, she didn't suffer one bit."

"I'm going to kill you when I get free," Kevin yelled.

"Say goodbye to your lovely wife," the killer said, aiming the gun at her head. He never got the chance as two bullets to the head sent her to the afterlife with her children.

As much as Kevin wanted to see this psychopathic killer on an autopsy table instead of rotting in a jail cell, he knew he wasn't in a place to compromise. His family had just been murdered in cold blood, and from the looks of things, he was surely about to be next. He had seen the killer somewhere before but just couldn't figure out where. Then it dawned on him.

"I know who you are. You're that re—"

"Shut up," the psychopath said, smacking him with the butt of the gun across the face. Blood instantly poured from the gash above his eye. "You don't know shit."

"The police will catch up to you and you will pay for this," Kevin stated, trying to figure out a way he could get some help.

"That's if they can catch me. I think my time is up here anyway," the killer replied. "You are the final piece to my puzzle."

"What are you talking about?"

"I'll show you exactly what I'm talking about." The killer pulled out a picture and showed it to Kevin. One look at the photo had him squirming in his seat. He turned his head away. "Isn't he so beautiful? This is the perfect soulmate."

"You're one sick motherfucker. Kill me, 'cause if I get loose, I'm surely gonna kill you."

"Oh, don't worry, that's definitely going to happen. I just wanted you to watch your family die first. I have to grab something. I'll be back."

Kevin waited for the killer to walk out and looked around for anything he could use to get himself out of this predicament. Knowing that he only had minutes to figure out something, he started rocking the chair until it fell over, bringing his wife down with him. Blood was everywhere! Still in pain from being hit with a gun, he tried wiggling out of the restraints again. He was almost out when the killer came back.

"I leave you alone for a couple of minutes and you try this. I guess this is goodbye then." With no remorse at all the killer aimed the gun at Kevin and shot him twice in the chest.

"Tell me what you want, Ashley."

"You," she gasped.

"Where?"

"Bed."

He broke free, scooping her into his arms, and carried her quickly and seemingly without any strain into her bedroom. Sitting her on her feet beside the bed, he leaned down to switch on the bedside lamp. He glanced around the room and hastily closed the curtains.

"Don't worry, my sister is out of town for the weekend, and I'm quite sure she wouldn't mind this," Ashley chuckled.

"I'm not worried at all," Eric said softly. "Now what?"

"Make love to me."

"How?" he teased. "You have got to tell me."

"For starters, you can undress me."

He smiled and stuck his index finger into her open shirt, pulling her toward him and slowly unbuttoning her blouse. Tentatively she put her hands on his arms to steady herself. He didn't complain a bit. In fact, ever since he had that threesome with her and Veronica, he had wanted some more. Guess you could say Ashley really had that good good. When he finished with the buttons, he pulled her shirt off and let it fall to the floor. Eric reached down to the waistband of her jeans, popped the button, and pulled down the zipper.

"Tell me what you want me to do to you, Ashley." His eyes smoldered and his lips parted as he took quick shallow breaths.

"Kiss me from here to here," she whispered, trailing her finger from the base of her ear, down her throat. He smoothed her hair out of the line of fire and bent, leaving sweet soft kisses along the path her finger was taking and back again.

"Now what?"

"My jeans and panties," Ashley murmurs. Eric smiled, dropping to his knees in front of her. It felt so good to her. Hooking his thumbs into her jeans, he gently pulled them, along with her panties, down her legs. Ashley stepped out of them, leaving her with only a bra on.

"Now what, Ash?" He stopped and looked up at her expectantly, but didn't get up.

"Kiss me," she whispered.

"Where?"

"You know where," she moaned, acting like she was a shy girl.

She pointed at the apex of her thighs, and he grinned wickedly. Ashley closed her eyes, mortified, but at the same time horny as fuck.

"Oh, with pleasure, my dear," he chuckled. Eric kissed her and unleashed his long, thick tongue. She groaned every time his tongue touched her body. He didn't stop though, as his tongue circled her clitoris, driving her insane. It kept going around and around, up and down.

"Eric, please," she begged, not wanting to cum standing. She didn't have the strength to hold on any longer. "I want to fuck right now."

He stood up, his lips glistening with the evidence of her arousal. Ashley started pulling off his clothes as he fondled her breasts. She dropped to her knees in front of him, yanking down his boxers. His ten-inch python sprung free from its captor. Eric watched as she took hold of him, squeezing tightly. He groaned and tensed up when she took him into her mouth, sucking and licking every inch. He cupped her head tenderly, and she pushed him deeper into her mouth, pressing her lips together as tightly as she could.

"Fuck," he hissed through gritted teeth. "Ash,

you made your point. I don't want to cum in your mouth."

She did it once more, and Eric bent down, grabbed her by the shoulder and pulled her up to her feet, and tossed her onto the bed. Ashley lay down, gazing up at him as he slowly positioned himself over her, licking his lips. He tore off her bra and kissed each of her breasts, teasing her nipples along the way. Gazing at her, he pushed her legs apart and slowly entered her steaming hot love box at a slow pace, before speeding up.

"Faster, Eric, harder . . . yes, just . . . like . . . that," she moaned, lifting her body in the air, giving him more access to drill her.

He gazed down at her in triumph, kissing her hard, and really started to dig into her walls. Her orgasm was building at a rapid pace, and her legs tensed up beneath him.

"Come on, baby," he gasped. "Give it to me."

His words made her explode, magnificently, mind-numbingly, into a million pieces all over him, and he followed up with his own explosion.

"Ash! Oh fuck, Ash!" He collapsed on top of her with his head buried in her neck. "Damn, your pussy is so fucking good. I can get use to this."

"What would my sister think if she heard you talking about my kitty kat like that?" Ashley joked. They both burst out laughing as Eric rolled off of her.

He was looking up at the ceiling when his cell phone went off. Already knowing who it was from the ringtone, he let it go straight to voicemail. Seconds later, it went off again.

"Somebody's trying to get in touch with you. You better get that."

"It's just work," Eric replied, rubbing her pussy. It instantly got moist again from his touch. She was ready for action again, until the phone went off again. This time he knew something was wrong because

Sonya would never call continuously like that. "Excuse me for a minute. Hello, Eric here."

"We have a major problem."

"What's wrong?" he asked, getting out of the bed.

"ADA Bachman hasn't been answering his phone for two days. Cynthia sent someone to his home, and they found his whole family murdered, including him. Eric, there was another horoscope quote written on his chest. I think we may have passed judgment on the wrong person. Our killer is still out there . . ."

To order books, please fill out the order form below:
To order films please go to www.good2gofilms.com
Name: _____
Address:_____
City: _____ State: _____ Zip Code: _____
Phone:_____
Email: _____
Method of Payment: Check   VISA   MASTERCARD
Credit Card#:_ _____
Name as it appears on card: _____
Signature: _____

Item Name	Price	Qty	Amount
48 Hours to Die – Silk White	$14.99		
A Hustler's Dream - Ernest Morris	$14.99		
A Hustler's Dream 2 - Ernest Morris	$14.99		
A Thug's Devotion – J. L. Rose and J. M. McMillon	$14.99		
All Eyes on Tommy Gunz – Warren Holloway	$14.99		
Black Reign – Ernest Morris	$14.99		
Bloody Mayhem Down South – Trayvon Jackson	$14.99		
Bloody Mayhem Down South 2 – Trayvon Jackson	$14.99		
Business Is Business – Silk White	$14.99		
Business Is Business 2 – Silk White	$14.99		
Business Is Business 3 – Silk White	$14.99		
Cash In Cash Out – Assa Raymond Baker	$14.99		
Cash In Cash Out 2 - Assa Raymond Baker	$14.99		
Childhood Sweethearts – Jacob Spears	$14.99		
Childhood Sweethearts 2 – Jacob Spears	$14.99		
Childhood Sweethearts 3 - Jacob Spears	$14.99		
Childhood Sweethearts 4 - Jacob Spears	$14.99		
Connected To The Plug – Dwan Marquis Williams	$14.99		
Connected To The Plug 2 – Dwan Marquis Williams	$14.99		
Connected To The Plug 3 – Dwan Williams	$14.99		
Cost of Betrayal – W.C. Holloway	$14.99		
Cost of Betrayal 2 – W.C. Holloway	$14.99		
Deadly Reunion – Ernest Morris	$14.99		
Dream's Life – Assa Raymond Baker	$14.99		
Flipping Numbers – Ernest Morris	$14.99		

Flipping Numbers 2 – Ernest Morris	$14.99		
He Loves Me, He Loves You Not - Mychea	$14.99		
He Loves Me, He Loves You Not 2 - Mychea	$14.99		
He Loves Me, He Loves You Not 3 - Mychea	$14.99		
He Loves Me, He Loves You Not 4 – Mychea	$14.99		
He Loves Me, He Loves You Not 5 – Mychea	$14.99		
Killing Signs – Ernest Morris	$14.99		
Kings of the Block – Dwan Willams	$14.99		
Kings of the Block 2 – Dwan Willams	$14.99		
Lord of My Land – Jay Morrison	$14.99		
Lost and Turned Out – Ernest Morris	$14.99		
Love & Dedication – W.C. Holloway	$14.99		
Love Hates Violence – De'Wayne Maris	$14.99		
Love Hates Violence 2 – De'Wayne Maris	$14.99		
Love Hates Violence 3 – De'Wayne Maris	$14.99		
Love Hates Violence 4 – De'Wayne Maris	$14.99		
Married To Da Streets – Silk White	$14.99		
M.E.R.C. - Make Every Rep Count Health and Fitness	$14.99		
Mercenary In Love – J.L. Rose & J.L. Turner	$14.99		
Money Make Me Cum – Ernest Morris	$14.99		
My Besties – Asia Hill	$14.99		
My Besties 2 – Asia Hill	$14.99		
My Besties 3 – Asia Hill	$14.99		
My Besties 4 – Asia Hill	$14.99		
My Boyfriend's Wife - Mychea	$14.99		
My Boyfriend's Wife 2 – Mychea	$14.99		
My Brothers Envy – J. L. Rose	$14.99		
My Brothers Envy 2 – J. L. Rose	$14.99		
Naughty Housewives – Ernest Morris	$14.99		
Naughty Housewives 2 – Ernest Morris	$14.99		
Naughty Housewives 3 – Ernest Morris	$14.99		
Naughty Housewives 4 – Ernest Morris	$14.99		
Never Be The Same – Silk White	$14.99		
Shades of Revenge – Assa Raymond Baker	$14.99		

Slumped – Jason Brent	$14.99		
Someone's Gonna Get It – Mychea	$14.99		
Stranded – Silk White	$14.99		
Supreme & Justice – Ernest Morris	$14.99		
Supreme & Justice 2 – Ernest Morris	$14.99		
Supreme & Justice 3 – Ernest Morris	$14.99		
Tears of a Hustler - Silk White	$14.99		
Tears of a Hustler 2 - Silk White	$14.99		
Tears of a Hustler 3 - Silk White	$14.99		
Tears of a Hustler 4- Silk White	$14.99		
Tears of a Hustler 5 – Silk White	$14.99		
Tears of a Hustler 6 – Silk White	$14.99		
The Last Love Letter – Warren Holloway	$14.99		
The Last Love Letter 2 – Warren Holloway	$14.99		
The Panty Ripper - Reality Way	$14.99		
The Panty Ripper 3 – Reality Way	$14.99		
The Solution – Jay Morrison	$14.99		
The Teflon Queen – Silk White	$14.99		
The Teflon Queen 2 – Silk White	$14.99		
The Teflon Queen 3 – Silk White	$14.99		
The Teflon Queen 4 – Silk White	$14.99		
The Teflon Queen 5 – Silk White	$14.99		
The Teflon Queen 6 - Silk White	$14.99		
The Vacation – Silk White	$14.99		
Tied To A Boss - J.L. Rose	$14.99		
Tied To A Boss 2 - J.L. Rose	$14.99		
Tied To A Boss 3 - J.L. Rose	$14.99		
Tied To A Boss 4 - J.L. Rose	$14.99		
Tied To A Boss 5 - J.L. Rose	$14.99		
Time Is Money - Silk White	$14.99		
Tomorrow's Not Promised – Robert Torres	$14.99		
Tomorrow's Not Promised 2 – Robert Torres	$14.99		
Two Mask One Heart – Jacob Spears and Trayvon Jackson	$14.99		
Two Mask One Heart 2 – Jacob Spears and Trayvon Jackson	$14.99		

Two Mask One Heart 3 – Jacob Spears and Trayvon Jackson	$14.99		
Wrong Place Wrong Time – Silk White	$14.99		
Young Goonz – Reality Way	$14.99		
Subtotal:			
Tax:			
Shipping (Free) U.S. Media Mail:			
Total:			

Make Checks Payable To: Good2Go Publishing, 7311 W Glass Lane, Laveen, AZ 85339

CPSIA information can be obtained
at www.ICGtesting.com
Printed in the USA
LVHW021704280120
645066LV00016B/1082

9 781947 340428